in the

DARK,

in the

WOODS

ELIZA WASS is a freelance writer, editor and journalist. She comes from Southern California, where she was one of nine perfect children with two perfect parents. She has thousands of friends, all of whom either arrive inside dust jackets or post obsessively on Twitter.

Eliza spent seven years in London with the most amazing man in the world, her late husband Alan Wass, of the band Alan Wass and The Tourniquet, who inspired her to pursue her dreams and live every day of her life.

@Lovefaithmagic

in the
DARK,
in the
WOODS

ELIZA WASS

Quercus

QUERCUS CHILDREN'S BOOKS

First published in the US by Hyperion,
125 West End Avenue, New York, New York 10023

This edition published in Great Britain in 2016 by Hodder and Stoughton

1 3 5 7 9 10 8 6 4 2

A CIP catalogue record for this book
is available from the British Library.

PB 978 1 78429 991 0

Printed and bound in Great Britain by Clays Ltd, St Ives plc

The paper and board used in this book are
made from wood from responsible sources.

MIX
Paper from
responsible sources
FSC® C104740

Quercus Children's Books
An imprint of
Hachette Children's Group
Part of Hodder and Stoughton
Carmelite House
50 Victoria Embankment
London EC4Y 0DZ

An Hachette UK Company
www.hachette.co.uk
www.hachettechildrens.co.uk

This book is dedicated to Alan Wass

You made a blind man see,
You made a man out of me,
And if you go away on your own,
Please don't be too long,
I will be waiting here patiently,
From the moment you're gone.

— "From the Moment You're Gone"
Alan Wass and the Tourniquet

I carved my first star when I was six, so by the time I was sixteen there were stars everywhere in the woods. Some of them I didn't even remember carving. Sometimes I wondered if someone else had—Hannan or Delvive or Caspar or Mortimer or Jerusalem. Or my other brother, the one who died. But I think I knew it was just me. I think I knew I was the only one carving stars.

one

At three o'clock Sunday morning, I was balanced on the apex of Ms. Sturbridge's roof, watching my brother upturn bundles of wet leaves with a stick. Ms. Sturbridge was in the hospital, so there was no chance of anyone hearing us cleaning her rain gutter, but Caspar kept quiet. We had to work at night so they wouldn't see us. Caspar said he wanted it to be a surprise, but really he didn't want Father to find out.

I tipped my head back and narrowed my eyes at the stars. "Do you want to hear something completely disturbing I found out at school?" I knew he didn't—completely disturbing wasn't really Caspar's thing—but he was also a good listener, so he just said, "Tell me," and carried on with his work.

"You know Cassiopeia is supposed to be *my* constellation?" Father had given each of us a constellation, as if they belonged to him personally. Caspar didn't nod or anything, because he didn't like where I was going. "Well, basically, in Greek mythology, Cassiopeia was punished for being vain, and her punishment was to be tied to a chair in the sky. So that's where she is, up there in the sky, tied up. And that's *my* constellation."

Down below I heard Mortimer, my other brother, whoop. He was supposed to be keeping watch. "You do realize that's not really the queen of Ethiopia up there in the sky?" he called. "You do realize the Greeks made that shit up?"

"Yeah, but Father calls it Cassiopeia, too," I said. "So clearly he's aware of it."

"You're right—what is it Father says? 'The Word has many meanings.' I'm pretty sure he's trying to tell us something. I'm pretty sure he wants us to tie you to a chair."

"Like I would notice the difference," I said under my breath, so only Caspar heard.

His eyes went all wide. That was one thing that bothered me about Caspar. Whenever anyone expressed frustration, he was surprised—I mean, *really shocked*, like it never occurred to him.

"Castley, this is just a waiting period. Things will be better in heaven," he said gently. God must have been kidding when he gave Caspar a voice, because even though Caspar looked like a saint, and was by far the prettiest of all of us, girls included, when he spoke he sounded like a construction worker on two packs a day, in a way that made girls go absolutely crazy. Not that he noticed.

"I don't want to wait. I want things better now."

I heard Mortimer scurrying up the drainpipe to join us. The little rat. Mortimer was pretty much an albino, so he got it worse from the townsfolk than anyone. He also gave it worse than anyone, which was generally how it worked.

"I don't know why you think anyone has it better than we do," Mortimer said, climbing up onto the roof. "Life sucks for everyone."

"Well, I would happily trade lives with any of them. Being 'blessed with the truth' is pretty much a pain in the butt."

Caspar braced himself. Maybe I'd gone too far. He dropped down so the roof fluttered beneath our feet.

"Caspar? What is it?" I thought he'd dropped into an emergency prayer or something.

"There's someone down there," he breathed. My first

3

instinct was to not believe him, which just goes to show how many times I'd been tricked, but then a light shot along the roof and up over our heads. Mortimer dove down, lying flat against the rooftop. Heavy feet crunched through the dried grass, and I hesitated.

"Castley, get down!" Mortimer said. He was probably embarrassed about how quickly he'd gone down.

A light hit the chimney, where it turned into a yellowing circle. It bounced lightly, then slithered along the apex of the roof, toward me.

They might see me, I thought, and stupidly, I wanted to be seen. I wanted it so badly, I guess I didn't care how it happened. I felt a hand on my wrist, and Caspar grabbed me, pulling me down beside him.

"Is someone there?" It was an old man's voice and it snapped me out of my stupor. It wasn't a white knight or a prince or even just a teenage boy come to rescue me.

I clung to Caspar, scared now, and felt his heart race through his secondhand clothes.

"Hello? Is there someone up there or what?" he said, like we were keeping him in suspense. A dog howled, way out across the field, and the man said, "Probably just rats," and shuffled away through the grass.

We stayed frozen for a long time, Mortimer sprawled

like a doll across the roof and Caspar beside me, watching the sky. Mortimer sat up. He screwed up his big lips and licked his teeth, flinching slightly. "Nice one, Castley. He almost saw you."

"But he did see *you*." I extracted myself from Caspar. "You heard him: 'just a rat.'"

"He said 'just rats.'"

"Maybe you all should go home," Caspar said abruptly. We both turned. Our jaws dropped, as if we couldn't believe he didn't want us there. Neither of us was helping any. We had both offered to keep watch, and we had failed even at that.

"Caspar . . ." I started. He scooped up his stick and drove it into the rain gutter, turning up gunk that fell in wet bundles to the ground below. *They'll probably think the rats did it. Rats, or maybe God. I suppose that's what Caspar wants.*

"Come on, Castley. Let's go." Mortimer slid down the roof toward the drainpipe. Although they were pretty much exact opposites, Mortimer had a weird respect for Caspar.

I looked at Caspar. Maybe if I really helped, he would let me stay. I could find my own stick, or I could just pull leaves out with my bare hands.

5

Caspar was obsessed with doing good things for the people in town: the people who hated us, who mocked us, who said terrible, disgusting things about us. Caspar liked to sweep their porches or pull their weeds or clean their windows. I wasn't quite so enamored with them. "Fine," I said. "We'll go."

I climbed down the drain after Mortimer. The pair of us kept quiet as we followed the fence that separated the Sturbridge farm from the Higgins farm. When we reached the woods, we both spoke at once.

"You shouldn't test Caspar like that—"

"Do you think it'll be warm enough to go swimming tomorrow? Wait—what do you mean, test him?"

"I mean holding on to him like that." He forced a branch aside.

"What are you talking about? I was scared!"

"I'm just trying to do you a favor. Don't act like you don't know what I'm talking about."

I wanted to say something, but I didn't, for the same reason I always kept quiet: because I could never be sure of what they thought, not any of my brothers and sisters. I could never be sure of how much they believed—I wasn't even sure how much *I* believed—because Father believed a lot of crazy things.

Father taught us that we were the only pure people left on earth, we were the only worthy people, and because of that, we would all have to marry one another. Not in a civil ceremony or anything, which would be illegal, but in a heavenly ceremony. And I was supposed to marry Caspar. Delvive was paired with Hannan, and poor, sweet Jerusalem was stuck with Mortimer.

When I was younger, I honestly thought securing Caspar was a real score. *Lucky me, I got the pretty, nice brother!* Then Momma's accident happened and we were forced to go to a real school, and I found out that not only was it illegal to marry your brother, but it was also totally disgusting.

The six Cresswell children, bound together for all eternity. It was too perfect, except . . . I used to have an older brother. His name was also Caspar. He was born before us triplets (Delvive, Hannan, and me), but he died. And the *new* Caspar, the one I was supposed to marry someday, was actually a reincarnation of the one that came before.

I shivered in the cold. "School starts tomorrow." I didn't really know what else to say about it. I had learned not to get too excited about school.

"Yup," Mortimer said, licking his teeth.

"Is there something wrong with your mouth?"

Mortimer bristled, pushing ahead through the trees. "No."

"Because you keep messing with it. You keep pushing your tongue around between your teeth, like you've got something in there."

"And what exactly would I put in there, dear sister? A suitcase? A very small umbrella?"

I laughed in spite of myself and hurried to catch up. "I don't know; I thought maybe you cut your lip or something." His eyes traced my face, reading it for clues. "You can tell me, you know. I'll never tell." That was only lately true. I was a real tattletale growing up; we all were. There was a competition between us. *If Father loves your brothers and sisters less, then he loves you more.*

Mortimer pursed his lips, then flinched in pain.

"I swear on Momma's life, I won't say anything," I said. It was a pretty serious thing to swear on, because almost as long as she'd been alive, Momma had been on the brink of death.

Maybe that was why Mortimer stopped, leaning against the trunk of a tree so one of my stars hung over his shoulder. Mortimer had huge lips; they were his only beautiful asset—swollen and pouty and berry-colored.

He took his top lip in his fingers and rolled it up like a curtain, and inside a red bulb burned, hot and painful-looking.

"Oh my God. What happened? Did Father—"

He released his lip. "No, Father didn't do it to me, you idiot. But I'm scared as shit he's gonna find out."

"What is it—like, herpes?" I said. He shoved himself off the tree and plunged ahead through the woods. "Oh my God. Did you catch it from somebody?" He actually growled, so I tried to collect my cool. Of all my brothers and sisters, Mortimer was the last one I would ever expect to kiss someone. Not just because of the way he looked, but because he actively hated pretty much everyone. "Oh my God! Who did you kiss?"

"Stop saying oh my *you-know-what*!" That was the kind of thing that confused me about my brothers and sisters. The way they flouted some rules and upheld others at the same time. Mortimer had just confessed to kissing someone, and yet there he was, attacking me for taking the Lord's name in vain.

"Wow. If Father finds out, you're in so much trouble. Like, I can't even imagine how much trouble." He rushed through the trees. We were almost home. I reached out to stop him. "Wait! I'm sorry. Maybe I can help you."

"How?" he snapped, but he still pulled up, fidgeting with his hoodie.

"You can buy cream for that. It'll make it less painful, make it heal faster." Father didn't believe in modern medicine—not that he'd have handed out ointment to a kissing little sinner anyway. I tried to look considerate, but I wanted to know who Mortimer had kissed so badly that I could feel it pushing against the tips of my fingers.

"Oh yeah? You gonna buy that for me?"

"No. But I could steal it."

His pupils expanded, black inside his muddy gray eyes. "Castley."

"What's the problem? I never get caught. I know you do, but I'm smart, I'm careful. I'll steal it for you. I'll do it today."

"It's Sunday. The pharmacy's closed."

"They'll have it at the Great American. They have everything at the Great American."

He swiped the sore with his tongue. "Castley, you won't be able to get away with it at the Great American. They know who we are; every place in town does. We have a bad reputation for thieving."

"Thanks to you."

He scoffed. "I didn't hear you complaining all those

times I brought you chocolate, or that steak we cooked out in the woods."

"That was the best." I smiled. "So you see, I owe you. I at least want to try. I'm not afraid of them, anyway."

"It's not them I'm worried about."

Right then the house appeared, waiting for us, dressed in shadows, clothed in rotted wood. I hated our house more than anywhere else on earth. Every hallway, every corner, every little nook, had a memory. If I stared at any one spot for too long, I risked dropping down inside one, drowning in a memory until I came up screaming.

I hovered on the edge of the woods. My mind skied over the usual thoughts. *You could just leave. You could just leave and never come back.* But then a million and one thoughts rushed in, like dirt chases a broom. *You're not old enough. You have to be able to support yourself to be emancipated, and you don't have any friends or family. If you went to child services, if you told on him, your entire family would turn against you. You still love him.* And, worst of all, *What if he's right?*

None of these thoughts ever left my head. I kept a close watch on them, stifling them, shoving them down when they came too close to the surface.

There were some things you could never say because, the moment you did, you changed *everything*.

I bounced on my heels. "What time is it?"

"Um, I don't know; five?"

"Why don't we just go now, before prayers?" We had prayers every morning at six thirty. I didn't see the point in going home right then. It's not like we would sleep. We all had trouble sleeping, except for Hannan, who forced himself for football's sake. The rest of us slept in fits and bursts, tossing and turning. I think we knew how much we were missing and it kept us up at night. I think we were afraid of missing more.

Mortimer shook his head. "We won't make it back in time."

"It's only two miles from here. That's twenty minutes, tops. It's perfect. It won't be busy."

"It's better if it *is* busy. If you don't want to be seen."

"Nobody ever sees me. I practically don't exist."

Mortimer made a face, but when I turned, he followed me. I walked faster. I focused on not thinking about what would happen, on not planning. Because if you planned, you would only be disappointed. If you tried to force the future, it never worked out the way you pictured it. Father taught me that. By planning everything, he taught me that.

12

One day I wanted my life to be wide open. I wanted to live without a map. I wanted everything, even the road I was walking on, to disappear, so that for once I didn't have to know where I was going.

That was what I focused on: possibility. And I wasn't afraid. And when the Great American appeared, I thought I was ready for it.

"Stay here," I told Mortimer. Instead of making a face or groaning, he curled behind a tree and watched me go.

two

The Great American was a gas station convenience store just off the main highway leading into Almsrand. The sky was lightening overhead, but the parking lot was deserted. Lupe sat behind the counter, staring at a fixed point in space with his head tipped back, like he was putting himself in a trance.

I honestly thought that I could walk right in and he wouldn't even see me. That was about how real I felt in that town. Most people, the so-called "good people," looked the other way when we crossed the street, like my teachers never looked me in the eye when they noticed my wrists were bruised, like boys bumped into me in the hall and then scowled at the space above my head and hurried away. Delvive and I did Drama, and I swear, even when we did our scenes, even when we were the only two people on stage, our fellow classmates still managed not to see us.

So I thought I could walk into the Great American invisibly.

I crossed the parking lot. As I hit the sidewalk, I tried to avoid my reflection in the windows—pale, graying skin, shapeless cotton shift dress, frizzy hair knotted up in an elaborate braid. In my mind I looked so different than I did in real life that sometimes seeing myself shocked me.

I dropped my chin and continued to the door. I pushed it open and the bell rang (at least I think it did), but Lupe never looked up. I bowed behind an aisle, chasing the magazine rack to a small health section. I crouched down, tucking my knees up under my dress. I skimmed over condoms and tampons and Deep Heat.

Antiviral cream. I grabbed it when the doorbell rang— once, twice, and then four more times. I saw their feet first, a train of multicolored Ugg boots, and I knew they were girls my age. When you were living a life you hated, there was absolutely nothing worse than the people who were living the life you wanted. Still, I couldn't stop myself from looking.

I leaned back, careful but curious, until I caught Riva's

leering grin. She was dressed in a onesie. They all were—Riva and Lisa and Darla and Emily Higgins and a black girl I didn't recognize—in bright, crazy colors with funny patterns, as though clothing could be purchased as a punch line. They all had pink streaks in their hair; they must have done them together. They must have just come from a sleepover.

"Lupe!" Riva squealed. Riva wasn't popular, but she did all the things that popular people were supposed to do, like she thought that eventually people would just shrug and start to worship her. "We're gonna make pancakes! Do you have pancake stuff?!" Everything she said seriously ended in an exclamation point.

Lupe put on this big, goofy grin and started trailing them around the store like he couldn't get enough of her shrill squeal.

"Lupe! Where's the good kind?! This isn't the good kind! The one with the horse on it! Remember?! I love that one! Lupe, it's my birthday! Guess how old I am! Not old enough for you!" The other girls talked, too, but there was no way of knowing what they said with Riva there.

I should have made a run for it. It was the perfect opportunity. Caspar would've called it a "blessing," like he called every good thing (although he never breathed a word when bad stuff happened). Lupe had left the counter. The path to the door was obstruction-free.

Instead I felt myself wither. I felt myself crouching down, hand curling around the packet, as though I might just take the opportunity to dissolve into the shop floor. I didn't even notice them behind me.

"Hey!" Lisa said. She stepped back quickly, bumping into the new girl, who stood behind her.

The girl's hair was braided in a halo around her head. Something about the way she carried herself made me shrink even further.

"I know you," she said. I was sure I'd never met her in my life.

Lisa took in the antiviral cream clutched in my sweaty hand, and I felt my neck, my face, my eyelashes, go red. She frowned. "I thought you guys didn't believe in modern medicine," she said, as though I were a sociological experiment.

"Hey! Lisa! Amity! Who are you talking to?!" Riva appeared at the other end of the aisle (*it's a trap!*) with her little army falling in behind her. "Oh my God! You are shitting me!"

My mind went blank. It's called sheer panic. I needed to get out of there, but I couldn't run past Riva with the

17

antiviral cream. She'd think I had herpes or some other gross disease. Plus I hadn't exactly planned on paying for it.

I chucked the cream into the shelf, knocking condoms and tampons and Deep Heat across the floor. Then I sprinted, actually sprinted, toward the door.

I shoved past Riva as she swore and put her arms out to catch me. I raced across the parking lot, past Riva's mother waiting in her Range Rover. I heard them all laughing. I heard Riva and her exclamation points sending them all into fits of giggles.

Mortimer tried to grab me as I ran past. "Did you get it?" I kept running. I heard his footsteps pound behind me. "Castley! Did you get it? Did someone catch you? Is someone following us?" His footsteps slowed, but I kept running. I ran even faster. "Castley!" he called, but in the end he just let me run. I ran and I ran, until I was good and alone.

The one nice thing about our house was that it was easy to sneak in and out of, because it was so big.

I reached the yard and checked that the coast was clear. Then I hesitated, stalking the edge of the woods surrounding the house. It couldn't be six yet, and I didn't want to go back to my room, where I would no doubt be questioned as to my whereabouts by Delvive, my triplet sister. I wondered if Caspar was back yet. I thought maybe I would just wait for him, so I sat down in the dirt and wrapped my arms around my knees.

Sometimes in the woods, if I closed my eyes, if I really concentrated, I could make it so everything fell away. I would shiver first, usually, like I was dropping a heavy backpack. And then I would feel light everywhere, piercing through the pink skin of my eyelids. And when I opened my eyes again, the light would still be there, for a while at least. I used to think the light was God.

I tried to do it then, but I couldn't catch any light, just a milky darkness that made me feel cold and afraid.

I heard footsteps. Their pattern was sloppy, uneven, panicked. Mortimer was racing toward me. In his hand was a familiar white packet. His hoodie was torn, so it flopped loosely at his side. He skidded to a stop in front of me, dropping to his knees.

"You just got me in so much fucking trouble!" He clutched the packet to his chest.

"What are you talking about? I didn't do anything."

Mortimer grabbed my wrist. His eyes were wild. "Lupe called the cops. Officer Hardy had me by the fucking arm."

He held up his sleeve. The torn fabric dangled. My heart bounced against the ice that surrounded it.

"He won't do anything," I said. "He won't come out here. Not after what happened last time. Remember what they said? They need evidence."

"This isn't about Father, this is about me. Castley, I stole from the shop. Lupe saw me. I'm pretty sure—there were a bunch of girls from our school leaving as I went in."

"Those girls are idiots." I groaned, pressing my palms against my temples. "God, I told you; why do you always get caught?"

He staggered to his feet. "You're not helping." He paced in front of me, threading his fingers through his hair in agitation. "I can't believe this is happening."

"Mortimer, the police never do anything. For anything to happen, they'd have to admit we exist, and you know that's not going to happen."

"It's not the police I'm worried about."

My heart rattled in its cage. *If Father found out* . . .

"But he won't find out. How would he? It's not like he talks to anyone in town."

"Where's Caspar?" Mortimer said. "I need to speak to Caspar."

I scanned the trees. "I don't know where he is. I haven't seen him go in."

Mortimer pressed his torn sleeve together, as though it might magically repair itself. "Maybe I should go back toward the Sturbridge farm. See if I can catch him."

"Mortimer, I really don't think the police will do anything. Seriously. It's going to be fine."

He lurched away. "Yeah. Whatever. Thanks a lot."

"How is something you did *my* fault?" I called at his retreating form. "You're your own person! The decisions you make are yours!" He didn't acknowledge me.

What an idiot. What an idiot to go into the Great American right after I'd made a huge hullabaloo. It served him right, but if Father found out . . .

I steadied myself on a tree trunk. The house seemed to rise up before me, dark and full of secrets. I didn't want to go back in there. No. I wouldn't go back there now. I turned on my heel and hurried toward the Sturbridge farm.

The early morning light wept through the trees as I hurried through the woods. I loved the woods; I couldn't help it. They were free and wild and beautiful—everything I wasn't. In my dreams, I was the woods. In reality, I was . . . I couldn't even think of anything that fit.

I let myself drift a little, counting stars, remembering the days I'd carved them. I heard movement up ahead.

"Morty?" I called out, feeling my chest tighten. I was sure Mortimer would continue to blame me for what happened, my dear brother, even though it was in no way my fault he'd been born a complete idiot.

"Cass? Is that you?" Caspar broke through the trees, looking all angelic and heavenly as usual. Cain and Abel, my good and wicked brothers. "What are you doing out here?" He reached up and slid a briar from my hair.

"Did you see Mortimer? He was looking for you." I fell into step beside him.

"No."

"I think he might be in trouble."

"How do you mean?" Caspar twisted his pouty lips. His lips weren't huge like Mortimer's, but they had a heaviness that made him look stupid and sexual at the same time.

I told him what happened, leaving out the part where I went in first. Basically, I lied, but Caspar got the point.

We reached the edge of the woods. I knew it must be time for prayers because Caspar was like clockwork about those things. I hung back, dipping behind trees. The woods were like a safe zone for us, a place where we could be honest, a place where we could be ourselves. Once we crossed the tree line to go to school or to go home, the entire game changed. "What should we do?"

Caspar's brow furrowed. He had that look on his face, the look he got sometimes, like he was having a conversation with his own personal angel. "Get inside, before it's too late," he said, which didn't really answer my question, and then he turned back and went into the woods.

I had to be very careful going in. It was late enough in the morning that everyone would be up. If Momma'd had a rough night, Father might be in the kitchen making one of his "medicinal" potions.

I crept across the backyard, hiding behind the outhouse and the storage shed as I went. There was an overturned bucket beneath the kitchen window, but it wasn't noticeable, because the backyard—like most of the house—was a real mess. Father had an obsession with not wasting stuff, and since we never bought any "stuff" ourselves, that meant other people's stuff. Stuff he found on the side of the road when he drove around in his truck like a junkman, saving the world from waste.

The back shed and the porch and the yard were full of junk. We made money fixing it up to sell. Father would drive out to weekend markets, usually with Caspar because he was nice to look at and didn't complain, and sometimes with Baby J because she would just plop down anywhere and paint and people loved to watch her.

People loved Baby J. They loved her real name, Jerusalem. They loved that she was tiny and sort of serene. They loved that she never spoke; people thought that was really fabulous. "How wonderful," they would say, "that she can speak so beautifully through her paintings." What people didn't realize was that Baby J could speak, the same way they or any of us could. Even the people at school didn't seem to remember that she spoke, up until the age of six, the same year Morty broke his collarbone and the police raided our house.

The kitchen window was always open a crack so we could get in from the outside. I scanned the kitchen first, holding my breath and trying to feel the house for people.

Then I hurried. I stuck my pinkie into the space and lifted the window until I could fit my hand in. I raised the window slowly so it didn't stutter along the frame. I bounced on the bucket, feeling the give that would one day crack, and vaulted into the kitchen sink.

I scurried to the floor as quickly as I could. I had to be careful because there were buckets of water everywhere on the kitchen floor, like the world's wettest chess game. That was another thing Father fixated on: preparation. He hoarded tap water until it started to smell and had to be changed.

I guess it made sense in our house, where the plumbing was always going funny and we only had one working toilet, which we were only allowed to use at night and, even then, only in "emergencies" (otherwise we had to use the outhouse). Father didn't believe in plumbers. He thought when the plumbing went wrong, it was God's way of testing us and we had to endure.

I was dancing through the buckets when the kitchen door swung open. I froze, feeling the funny, airy wash of fear. I ran through excuses. I could say I had to use the outhouse, but that would implicate the window. I could say I wanted water. Yes. And if he asked why I didn't use the sink upstairs, I could say it tasted gross, which it did.

Only it wasn't Father who came through the door. It was Hannan, who looked the most like Father and gave me a pretty good fright anyway.

"Jeez! What are you doing?" He rubbed his eyes.

"I was getting water," I said before I realized he probably didn't require an answer.

He passed by me, swerving expertly through the

buckets on the floor, until he reached the cupboard. I made for the door.

"Hey!" he said. I spun around. He held out a cup.

"Oh," I said dumbly. He went to the sink to fill it up for me.

Hannan, Delvive, and I were triplets, but of all my brothers and sisters, even Jerusalem, Hannan was the hardest to figure out. He was the high school quarterback—he was actually amazing at playing football—and all he ever did was eat, sleep, and practice. I couldn't tell what he thought about anything, Father or school or life in general. The only interesting thing he'd ever done was walk Claire, the head cheerleader, home from school. When Father found out, it earned Hannan a week in the Grave.

The Grave was a cave underneath a stone amphitheater out in the woods. It was kind of like a sewer, and it was built to drain the overflow from the rain and the snow, but according to Father, it was put there by God as a place of reflection. Generally this reflection was enforced.

Hannan had been in the Grave once, and Mortimer had been a lot. Caspar went down there voluntarily whenever he suspected himself of doing wrong or thinking wrong and he wanted to get a head start on his punishment. Sometimes Caspar would stay out there for days, without food, which made Father positively gleeful. I guess because it proved Father right. It proved that it couldn't be so bad to be locked in a sewer, without food or water, in the middle of the woods with only God for company (if God thought you were worth sticking around for). It couldn't be so bad if a kid was literally volunteering.

None of us girls had ever been in the Grave, not because Father thought we were sensitive or anything, but because we'd never been caught doing wrong. We were smart. And we were way too smart to volunteer.

I thanked Hannan as he handed me the water, all the while wondering if he knew I'd been outside or if he really thought I was dumb enough to go get water without remembering to get a glass. I didn't ask him because that was how we interacted inside the house. We were putting on a performance all the time, because someone was always watching.

I held my water glass close and hurried up the stairs. I didn't want to be the first one down and risk Father having a personal chat with me.

Delvive and Baby J and I all shared a room. There were enough bedrooms in the house for each of us to have our own room and then some, but there was also no central heating. So we three girls shared a room and so did the three boys.

Our room was decorated with dead flowers, which hung on strings that crossed and crisscrossed like a bridal web. When I went in, Delvive and Baby J were sitting Indian style on the floor, with Baby J in front and Delvive behind braiding her hair.

"Morning," I said. Baby J turned to smile, but Del jerked her head back into place.

I put the water glass down and settled in behind Del and began to fix her hair, which had gone all frizzy in the night. Baby J would do mine once hers was finished.

We faced the window, and every so often a tree shivered, and I wondered if it was Caspar or Morty coming home, or running away.

three

We three sisters walked downstairs together. We stuck together as much as we could, not just at home, but at school, too. There was safety in numbers. Father was in the living room when we arrived, reading from his book in that posed way he had, as though he knew someone was watching and thought they might want to have a pretty picture.

Momma was in the corner. I could tell just by looking at her that it was a bad day. She was pale and she had her arms folded tight around her. My mother had once been the most beautiful woman in the world, and I'm not exaggerating. She was like a doll: white-blond hair like Morty, blue eyes like Caspar, ethereal like Delvive. But she had aged like a doll. Her features were chipped and worn down. Worst of all was her right leg, which was bent sideways.

She had broken it falling down the stairs. She never went to the hospital. She refused to go. When it happened, she just looked at Father and said, "God will heal me, God will heal me," while her eyes said, *I know you're sorry*. But God made for a casual doctor, even with the help Father gave him—the rudimentary splint and the potions and the healing blessings. Her leg never again looked like the leg God gave her, and she never walked again.

Of this fact she often seemed proud, as though it proved something about her character, about her faith, about her love for Father, which was worth more than walking through the woods, or running through the fields, or swimming through the lake.

We three girls filed in, heads bowed, and took our places—Baby J on the couch next to Hannan, and Del and me on the floor at their feet. Caspar and Mortimer still weren't back.

Father looked up from his book. "Hannan, where are your brothers?"

Hannan must have known about our nighttime activities, but he never took part. Still, he only said, "They're not upstairs, sir."

"Did you see them go out?"

"No, sir. I was asleep."

Father scanned his book, as if checking its opinion on the subject, then slid it shut. "Does anyone know where Mortimer and Caspar have gone?"

I kept my eyes trained on the floor, not trusting myself to look up. Father claimed that God would tell him if we were lying, but in this task God could be unreliable, so I decided not to help him along.

"Castella?" he said. My heart thudded. My mouth dried and my jaw groped. "Delvive? Jerusalem?"

He said their names, too, but he'd said mine first, mine first when Delvive was a few minutes older than me and should have gone before me. Did that mean God had told him? Did that mean he knew?

My upper lip was wet. My throat was dry. My breath echoed in the vacuum of my skull.

"Hannan. I'm disappointed in you. You share a room with your brothers. You are second eldest, and it is yours to keep watch over them." Father called Hannan second eldest even though the three of us—Hannan, Delvive, and me—were almost seventeen and Caspar was only fifteen. He called Caspar the eldest because he was the resurrected spirit of our older brother.

"I'm sorry, sir," Hannan said. When that didn't work, he added, "I'll strive to do better."

"How am I to begin when my children are missing? When my children are missing and one of them is lying?" I wasn't sure if he meant Hannan or if he knew it was me. My heart went fetal inside my rib cage. I kept my head down as my cheeks burned. Out of the corner of my eye, I saw Hannan glance at me.

"Hannan." Father moved toward us. "Is there something you would like to tell me?" Father's eyes went to me. Maybe God had told him, but it seemed more likely I had, with my clenched fists and my red face and my inability to meet his eye.

"I don't know, sir," he said. "This morning I found—" My eyes shot up. He wouldn't.

There was a knock on the front door. My heart uncoiled, so fast I practically sighed. Father stalked to the door.

I knew it was Mortimer and Caspar, but I didn't know what they would say, especially because Caspar refused to lie about anything.

Father led them back in. Mortimer's face was streaked with dirt and wavy salt lines like he'd been crying, although I couldn't imagine it. Caspar's invisible halo was still firmly in place as Father lined them up for the audience.

"Where have you been?" he asked Caspar, only Caspar, knowing Caspar wouldn't lie.

Caspar answered right away. "We were cleaning Ms. Sturbridge's rain gutter. It was my idea, sir." Pause. The air crackled, or maybe it was just in my mind. Was Caspar actually going to tell a lie? Was Caspar going to get Mortimer off? "Morty will tell you the rest." No such luck.

I stood up. If Caspar was too perfect to take the blame, then I would. "It was my fault. It was my idea to go to the Great American—"

Mortimer's face went white. I froze. He hadn't been planning on telling the truth; of course he hadn't. Caspar might not be willing to lie, but Mortimer would. And Caspar would let him. And I was a complete idiot.

Father's head cocked. Father was a frighteningly attractive man—or maybe he was just attractive, and the fear belonged to me. His muscles were taut like cords beneath skin that was too tight. His teeth were a milky glass, but just slightly too long, so his smile had a feral quality.

"The Great American," he sang out. That was the most magical thing about Father: his voice. When we were

33

young (and even when we were probably too old), he used to tell the most incredible bedtime stories—long, drawn-out fantasies with pure, virginal princesses and gallant knights and terrible, tempting demons that always managed to convince the hero to make a fatal error. They always ended badly—every one of his stories—and it was only after the raid, when we were forced to enroll in school, that I realized no other stories in the world ended that way. Only Father's.

That was what I thought about as he stood before me. That was what I told myself: *Tell a story. Lie.* I flinched, like the idea stung. My eyes stayed closed for too long and I felt dizzy.

My heart was pulsing inside my veins, sending out little heart signals on tiny boats that raced through my bloodstream. *Lie! Lie! Tell a lie! Tell a story! Tell a lie!*

If I didn't lie, I knew what would happen. I could see it: Father would grab Mortimer. Or he might just hit him outright, knock him sideways. Mortimer would crawl away on the floor, and Father would chase after him, hold his face down against the rotting wood and scream in his ear. Jerk his hands behind his back and yank him to his feet, whacking whatever part of his body was closest.

That was what would happen, exactly as it had happened before.

Say you did it.

Castella Rachel Cresswell. Tell the truth; God is watching.

I opened my eyes. I couldn't tell if Father had actually spoken, or if I'd just heard it as if he had. *Or maybe it was God.*

I forced my eyes to stay open so I would know whether Father was speaking or whether I was imagining it.

"Castella, tell your father what happened." He said that; I was almost sure of it.

I couldn't look at Mortimer. Couldn't look at Caspar. I felt something burning inside my chest, and I thought maybe it was my soul.

I thought I might pass out.

And then I saw it, creeping furry around my vision and then washing through my eyes: the light. I didn't know for sure if it was God, but I thought I'd better take the chance, just in case.

I shut my eyes, held the light in.

"I told Mortimer I would go to the Great American and steal him . . . steal him antiviral cream."

"And then what happened?"

I didn't feel afraid anymore, not with my eyes closed. The truth was a peaceful field, pulsing inside my mind. *The truth shall set you free.*

"There were girls from school there. And I guess I was ashamed, so I didn't take it."

I felt a hand close over my shoulder and I feinted sideways. Another hand closed over my other shoulder, and they both held me down.

"You did well," Father said. "You were tempted, but in the end you chose right."

I felt myself slip, stutter, as if I might float away. And then my soul came back. It filled me all the way to the toes of my sensible boots.

"And then what happened?"

I kept my eyes shut, but whatever spirit had overcome me, whether it was God or just fear of Father, was gone. I felt desperately human. I had to pee.

I knew that when I opened my eyes I would see Mortimer and Caspar there and I would feel guilty. Why had I done it? Why had I betrayed them? I lied in my mind all the time.

I knew that if I could see myself from outside myself, if I were out there watching, I wouldn't like myself. In my mind, I was strong and in control, but in reality I was . . . I was nothing like I was inside my mind.

"I don't know the rest," I said. "I ran home."

I opened my eyes as Father swiveled on his heel to face Mortimer.

"And then what happened?"

Mortimer looked at Caspar, not because he thought he might save him, but because, I think, in that moment, he wished he were Caspar.

"I stole it," Mortimer said with dead, dull eyes. "You always told us not to respect the law of man."

Father's eyes narrowed, like he didn't appreciate Mortimer's attempt to use his words to justify himself. "Have I not warned you about the dangers of the materials they market as medicine? Do you want your skin to burn and rot away? Do you want your flesh to become weak? Your bones to cripple and your stomach to turn to ash?" Father tended to overstate his point, but I felt a wash of relief. Nothing had happened. Mortimer was still standing there. Father didn't even seem angry. If anything, he seemed calm, poised. Maybe everything would be okay after all. "Mortimer." He bounced on his heel. "Why do you feel you have a need for antiviral cream?"

Shit.

Mortimer's face, which was ratlike to begin with,

shriveled to a point. Why had I mentioned *antiviral cream*? It was all my fault.

Mortimer opened his big mouth. "I guess I like the way it tastes."

"Stop!" I screamed, even though nothing had happened. Nothing except Father's right shoulder tightening. Or had I just imagined it? I shook my head to clear it. "It was for me. I wanted it. I asked for it. It was for me, I swear."

The eyes of everyone in the room were on me: Hannan's and Delvive's and Jerusalem's and Mortimer's and Momma's and Father's, and Caspar's, burning, the way a candle flares before you blow it out. And every single one of them knew I was lying.

"Mortimer, are you going to let your sister take the blame?"

"No, sir."

"Are you going to tell me the truth?"

"Yes, sir."

"Why do you feel you have a need for antiviral cream?"

"Because I'm an idiot."

"And you have a virus. Where?"

Mortimer's lip jerked. "Inside my mouth."

"And how did you get that virus?"

"I kissed Lisa Perez."

Father nodded wisely, judiciously, with that way he had, as if he knew it all before he was told.

I couldn't believe it. Lisa Perez? I'd seen her just that morning in the Great American. She was one of the prettiest girls in school and she was kissing Mortimer? I would have suspected Morty of lying, but it wasn't really the time.

Father put his hands behind his back and crossed the room in front of us. "You see, children, the rules that we have, the rules that I give you, have been put in place to protect you." He turned to Mortimer. "Does it hurt?"

"Not really."

"But enough that you were desperate to steal, to take medicines that I have warned you, time and again, are dangerous to your body and your soul. And what else have I warned you of, Mortimer? Have I warned you not to touch, not to look at, these creatures that roam around this earth, vile, disgusting, and now we see, carriers of the most abominable diseases? Mortimer, I want you to show your brothers and sisters what happens to those who touch, who kiss, who harbor lustful thoughts. Show them."

Mortimer exhaled through his nose and put his

39

hands on his mouth. Slowly he rolled up his lip to reveal the bright, aching sore. Father lunged, grabbing him by the lip and twisting. Mortimer screamed and fell forward.

"God has punished you for your sins, but your punishment will not end there, for God has whispered to me in my sleep of your sins and ordered me to punish you. You will go directly to his Chambers, where you will attend his mercy."

Mortimer whimpered, then screamed as Father jerked him forward by the mouth. Caspar shuddered. His eyes met mine.

I heard a rushing sound, louder and louder in my ears. I thought the whole world might be caving in.

"It's a car!" Caspar yelled. "Sir, it's a car engine!"

Father released Mortimer. His eyes flew to the window, where a blue truck approached, bouncing along the unpaved road. "What hell have you brought upon my family?" Father backhanded Mortimer across the cheek. Then he adjusted his collar and made for the door.

"Fuck!" Mortimer choked out, collapsing on the floor. He put his hand to his mouth and then pulled it away, observing the blood that pulsed from his swollen lips.

"Mortimer," Momma scolded weakly. All eyes drew

40

toward her corner. She sat half shrouded in darkness, with her bad leg cocked and her face a mask of pain.

"I'm s-s-sorry, Momma," Mortimer said, and then he began to sob. Only he wasn't really crying; no tears came out. I think, maybe, he was too scared to cry.

Caspar got down on the floor to comfort him, murmuring in his ear and rubbing his back. Hannan read his book—was it possible he'd kept reading the entire time? Del fussed with her hair. Baby J watched the window. I turned toward it.

Father walked down the dirt road, so he met the truck as far away from the house as he could. There were two figures inside the truck—one large and male and the other smaller, dark-skinned. Was that the girl from the Great American?

Mortimer stood up, shakily, and craned to see. "That's Michael Endecott," he said, rubbing his lip.

We all knew of Michael Endecott, although only Mortimer knew him personally. Father spoke of him all the time. He grew up with Father and Momma. He had been in love with my momma, but Father, and God, had won out in the end.

Michael Endecott was the one, according to Father, who had organized the police raid, the one who lied (*told the truth*) about our family to the police. The one who wanted to tear us apart, to separate us. Because he was jealous, Father said, jealous because God loved us more. Jealous because we were a perfect, beautiful family and God loved us best. Even if he had a funny way of showing it sometimes.

four

I wanted to apologize to Caspar, but I couldn't do it inside the house, where we had to follow the "house" rules. Caspar knew that, but it didn't stop him from giving me the cold shoulder while I sat in the living room reading the book of Father's revelations.

That was my punishment. I had to read the book until I found forgiveness, which would happen when Father sat beside me and I recited to him a verse or two that could, in a pinch, be applied to the situation.

Mortimer was put in the Grave, or what Father called "God's Chambers." Tomorrow was the first day of the new school year, but Father didn't care. Kissing Lisa Perez was probably the worst thing that Mortimer had ever done, and I didn't know how long he'd be punished.

I couldn't stop thinking about the kiss, trying to work out the when and how. We never saw anyone during summertime. Even Mortimer kept to the woods, except when he was petty thieving or "helping" Caspar. In fact, Mortimer had spent the better part of the summer inside the Grave. So much so that it almost seemed like he wanted to be down there.

I became convinced that he had discovered a way out and was pulling one over on us. So one afternoon, about midsummer, I went out to the Grave to check on him.

The Grave was accessed by a trapdoor that Father kept padlocked, but behind the stage there was a barred sewer grate, like the back window of an old-time jail. I sat down outside the grate to talk to Mortimer for a while. I asked him why, why was he always breaking the rules as if he wanted to be punished?

"I don't know," he said with a sigh, plucking the petals off the wildflower I'd brought him as a present. "I guess because I'm scared of what will happen if I do. I'm scared of being put down here."

"So you like to scare yourself?"

"No. Exactly the opposite. I do it because when I'm down here, that's the only time I'm not scared of being put down here." He smiled, the shadows from the bars slicing his face.

Now Mortimer was down there again and he was going to miss the first day of his sophomore year, maybe even the first week.

Caspar hadn't been punished for sneaking out and cleaning Ms. Sturbridge's drain, but knowing him, he'd volunteer for something horrific at any moment. If he were allowed, he would have gone down with Mortimer. He would have gone down with him every time.

My punishment wasn't really a big deal. It was Sunday, so we weren't allowed to do anything but read scriptures and pray anyway. The only difference was I was sitting in the living room instead of my bedroom (where I spent more time gazing out the window, daydreaming) and Father would check on me periodically.

We Cresswells read the Bible, but we also read Father's own book of revelations, which he'd written himself and was always adding to or taking away from.

I didn't mind the Bible. I didn't blame it for anything. It was a beautiful book, and sometimes when I was reading it, I swear I felt the spirit of God or the fire or the light. Other times it just seemed boring.

But my father's book was different. It was messy and disorganized. It was grammatically incorrect and often verging on incoherent. There were passages like this:

The stars are hungry for the Children of God. The cosmos are licking their lips. Bound to the universe. Tied to heaven. Kings in the NEW WORLD.

They stuck in my mind like a dirty story. Sometimes I read them over and over again, trying to dig out the meaning. Sometimes I suspected there wasn't one.

That evening Caspar went into Father's office and asked him to let Mortimer go to school. He said it was important that Mortimer didn't fall behind, but Father said that school didn't matter, that if it weren't for the wicked people in this town (who had forced us to enroll after the raid and after we failed every test they put in front of us), we wouldn't be going to school at all, and that what God had to say to Mortimer was more important anyway.

After nightfall, Father came into the living room, where I was reading in the dark. I had left the lamp off because I didn't have Father's permission to turn it on. He swanned across the room and settled beside me on the couch. I could feel his breath on my neck as he read over my shoulder. I tried not to flinch as he fingered my hair.

"What have you learned, my little Castella?" Sometimes Father could tug my heartstrings. When I was a

46

little girl, he appeared such a romantic figure to me: handsome, with that magical voice and a look of divine torture on his face. Sometimes, when I gazed into his graying eyes, it was easy to believe that God and the devil really were playing a treacherous game inside him, that he was some kind of warrior fighting dark shadows.

I took a deep breath and read him some dumb verse about God punishing the wicked, because I thought he would like that, and then I said, "I think God placed those girls from my school at the Great American to stop me from stealing. And even though I hate them and they tease me and make fun of me, I guess they remind me how lucky I am to have a family who loves me."

He ran his fingers down my back, as if my hair were loose and not tied up above my head. "That's wonderful, Castella. That's exactly right."

We all had to wake up very early on school days because Hannan had football practice before school and we had to have prayers and read scriptures before he left. After scriptures, we were allowed to decide whether we wanted to go to school early with Hannan or stay at the house.

That morning everyone went to school early. We were

stir-crazy after a summer spent in isolation. We were also nervous, with Mortimer being locked up.

We all marched through the woods in the dark of the pre-morning. Hannan rushed ahead, trying to put distance between us. Delvive kept close to me. She always stuck by me during school, which probably made people think we were weirder than we actually were, because we were two thirds of a triplet deal and we looked the same in all the wrong ways.

Del had a very censorious personality. If she ever said something, it was to point out something wrong. That morning it was my hair, which she said was too loose.

"I'm not saying it looks bad; it just looks lopsided," she said.

"Then I'll take it out!" I quickened my pace. I wanted to speak to Caspar. I wanted to apologize for yesterday. But it was impossible to do with Del scurrying along beside me like the insecurity police.

"You can't just take it out," she scolded. "You know you can't. You're not allowed."

I tripped over a root, sighed like it was her fault, then rolled around to face her. She stepped back, stumbling over the same root.

"Well, we can redo it," I said. "We have an hour before

school starts, so we can go down to the theater and you can redo it in the girls' dressing room, and I'm sure it will look amazing and not at all lopsided and we can all breathe a sigh of relief."

Caspar and Hannan were way ahead of us now, so when Del nodded and said, "Okay," as if it were a real load off her mind, I lifted up the hem of my homemade dress and ran after the boys.

Caspar looked worried when I pulled up beside him, but he was always puzzling over some sincere moral dilemma, so I didn't take it seriously.

"I'm really sorry about what I said yesterday," I whispered, not sure whether it was safe to let Hannan hear. "I should have kept my mouth shut."

"You didn't do anything wrong, Castley. If anything, you did the right thing."

"So you would have told?"

His lips crinkled. "You shouldn't really take me for an example."

"What do you mean? You're the best of all of us."

That only served to make his face more somber, which really proved my point. He lifted a branch for me to walk under.

Hannan was well ahead now, but still I kept my voice

down. "Are you all right? You seem upset about something."

"I have this funny feeling." He didn't elaborate.

"What? You mean like something's going to happen? I get that sometimes. Like I know something's coming. I wonder why that happens."

"No, it's not that. Not exactly. It's more like something has happened, that something's happened in me that's going to make something happen outside me." He took a deep, crackly breath, and I got this funny feeling he was talking about sex. But he wouldn't. Caspar would never. I shook my head. I must have got it wrong. I had sex on the brain, ever since I'd heard about Morty kissing Lisa Perez. Ever since I'd seen that absolutely disgusting sore inside his mouth. *That proves sex is gross and wicked.* But why didn't I really feel that way? Why did I feel all moody and bodiless when I thought about kissing? Kissing. Lips pressed together. Nerves on fire. And the release, the escape, the freedom of living inside a kiss.

I wonder if Morty thought it was worth it. As far as I knew, Mortimer was the only one of my brothers and sisters who had ever kissed anyone, although Hannan was kind of a wild card.

"I think that's how it happens, anyway," Caspar continued, philosophizing the way he always did, always avoiding the trap. "I think that's why people sometimes think they see the future. Because something changes in them *first*, and the world shifts to fill the space."

We had stopped walking, although I still felt myself moving, pushing toward something that was bigger, more beautiful.

"Where did Mortimer kiss Lisa—I mean, did he tell you?"

"On the lips."

"No." I felt myself blushing. Where on earth did Caspar think I thought they were kissing? My mind ran quickly over the places on my body, in a whoosh like a gust of wind. Only in my mind it wasn't Mortimer and Lisa kissing; it was me and a shadow, a face I couldn't see.

I tried to fill in the blank. I tried to picture boys from school that I'd had crushes on, but all of them had turned on me—making fun of my family or else ignoring me completely (I didn't know which was worse).

And Caspar will marry Castella.

But I didn't want to kiss Caspar. We were related. We looked the same in a lot of ways (although I wouldn't have minded looking more like him). And apart from being my own brother, Caspar was kind of a dork.

Still, I felt jealous that Caspar might one day crack and kiss someone. Jealous because I was sure tons of girls wanted to kiss him, and I doubted a single boy wanted to kiss me. And if I didn't kiss someone there on earth, then I would never kiss anyone. I doubted there was kissing in heaven. I'd better make sure to kiss Caspar before I died.

I almost chastised myself out loud. Suddenly I felt ridiculously, shamefully grateful that we were going to school. That was the kind of thought process that occurred when we spent too much time together, alone in the woods, where the only laws belonged to nature and the only rules to Father. I needed reality, whatever that was, to save me from a place that made me think I could fill the empty space inside me with my brother.

"No," I said again. "I meant where did they kiss, like, logistically—in the town? In the woods?"

Caspar batted a passing branch. "They kissed in the, uh . . ." Caspar always spoke clearly, so I knew whatever he was about to say bothered him enough to make him stammer. "They kissed in God's Chambers."

"What do you mean? How?"

Caspar pushed his hair back, looking dazed. "Uh. According to Mortimer, she kissed him through the grate."

"Oh my God."

Caspar blew out his lips. I didn't blame him. The thought was explosive. Our father had always taught us that God's Chambers was policed by God himself, that hidden within it was a pathway that led directly into heaven.

I wanted to say something, to say more. I wanted to dissect the entire scene: Mortimer locked in a dark but holy cave, Lisa Perez wandering through the woods, lost but then found. What did he say to her? What did she think? How did she feel? Did she get down on the ground? (She must have.) Did she crawl to him on her knees? Did she feel the cold steel of the bars on her cheeks as she kissed his enormous lips? What did it feel like? Did God see?

I had stopped in my tracks without realizing it. Caspar stormed ahead. He didn't stop or turn, even though he must have known I'd fallen behind.

I stayed there for a second, hung up on my own shadow. If Mortimer had done that, if he had really done that, shouldn't he have been burned alive? Shouldn't God have punished him, really punished him, with more than just a sore inside his mouth?

But Father doesn't know. If Father knew, it would all be over. I couldn't even imagine what he would do.

But God knew, and all God did was give Mortimer a cold sore.

Del and I didn't realize there was going to be a problem until we picked up our class schedules. We were supposed to pick them up during orientation week, but Father never let us go because it wasn't required, and we Cresswells only did the bare minimum in everything school-related. We were absent with startling regularity, so no one in the administration building even batted an eye when Delvive handed over the note saying Mortimer was sick.

Caspar disappeared, probably to get a head start on his homework or help one of the teachers set up a classroom. Jerusalem went down to the art shack because Mrs. Tulle always let her paint before school started. Del and I sat down in the brush behind the theater, which was always unoccupied because it smelled of the sewer, and compared schedules while Delvive rebraided my hair.

We were both juniors and both honor students, so we usually had the same schedule, although if we had one or two classes apart, it wasn't the end of the world. Unless it was our favorite class.

"Oh my gosh, Castley. We don't have Drama together," Delvive read over my shoulder.

"What do you mean?" I held up my schedule, which I'd hardly glanced at. We were both supposed to have Advanced Drama. We auditioned last year. Delvive and I had done Drama together since freshman year. It was our thing. We were always scene partners, even if it meant that one of us had to play a boy, because the thought of doing a scene with anyone else was absolutely terrifying. "That can't be possible."

"Look!" Delvive said, releasing my hair and snatching my schedule out of my hands. "You have Advanced Drama right now—first period. I have Advanced Drama third period. They must have split the class."

"It's fine." I adjusted my hair in the reflection of the glass doors. Now it looked lopsided to me. "We'll just go to Admin and tell them to change it. What do I have third period?"

Delvive made a face, dropping my schedule in her lap. "CPM 3." Group math. Almsrand High School let me switch to CPM freshman year, when I was failing Algebra. I did a lot better in CPM, not because I participated in the group or anything, but because all of the smart kids shared their answers with everyone else. "I'm in Calculus. You're going to have to change classes. You're going to have to take Calculus with me."

"I cannot take Calculus. I haven't even taken Precalculus."

"Castley, you have to."

The bell rang. "Shit."

"Cass, don't swear."

I stood up, nervously jerking my shapeless dress into place. "Well, it's too late to change it now. Let's just go to our first two classes, and then we can go talk to Admin during break." I knew that we could have gone to Admin right then, and we probably should have, but I couldn't take Calculus. It was impossible. There had to be another way. "Why can't you switch to my class?"

Delvive looked appalled. *"CPM?"* she repeated. Snob. "I'm sure we'll figure something out. We have to." She squeezed my hand. "I don't want to do Drama with anyone else. We need to be together."

She didn't mention the main reason. If Father found out we weren't partnered together, especially if we were partnered with a boy, we wouldn't be allowed to take Drama at all.

Advanced Drama was held in a room inside the theater called the black box. I recognized most of the students. There were only about twenty of us, so it would be easy for Delvive to switch to my class.

Mrs. Fein, the teacher, had us all sit in a circle while she went over the class schedule. Mrs. Fein was pretty lax about everything; there were even rumors that she went out drinking with some of her students, so we weren't even twenty minutes in before she announced that we could break into partners for the rest of the class.

"You'll be together for the entire semester," she said. "So make sure you choose wisely. It's probably not a good idea to choose your flavor of the month." She looked specifically at Michael Whitman, who had kissed every girl in Drama, except for Del and me and maybe Mrs. Fein, although I wouldn't swear on it.

Michael Whitman chose his flavor of the month anyway. Everyone paired off pretty quickly, because they all knew each other and all their little political games were pretty much mapped out. I didn't choose anyone. I was going to wait for Delvive, who would *have* to switch to my class.

Mrs. Fein would never have noticed my partnerless state. She wouldn't have noticed until the day I performed my scene sans partner, if it weren't for the freshman boy raising his hand.

"Mrs. Fein? Sorry. I don't have a partner." He scanned the class hopefully.

Mrs. Fein sighed. She'd been halfway back to her desk, probably to spend the remainder of class fielding important e-mails on Twitter, and obviously this was a huge inconvenience for her. "That's impossible. There are twenty students."

The freshman examined a scab on his elbow. "Yeah. No. I definitely don't have a partner."

Mrs. Fein's hands went to her hips. "Who doesn't have a partner?" I dropped my chin. "Do I really have to do this?" *Be invisible, be invisible, be invisible.* "Hold hands with your partner. Everyone. Hold hands with your partner."

The freshman found me first. He bunched his lips up and prepared to smile.

Mrs. Fein sighed. "Cresswell. Do you have a partner?" She didn't even know whether I was my sister or me; she didn't even bother to ask.

I curled my lip. "I do now."

five

The freshman was relieved to have me as a partner. I know because he told me. He also told me everything in his life that led up to that point.

"See, I don't actually know anyone in this class. You're not supposed to be in Advanced Drama as a freshman—although I think Mrs. Fein's son was, because *duh*—but I asked if I could audition because I want to be an actor. At first Mrs. Fein said no, but then I was, like, persistent, and she gave in. I mean, I don't care if I'm famous or anything. I care about the work." He waited like this required a response. "Sorry. I forgot to ask. What's your name?"

We were sitting in a quiet section of the theater alcove, away from the madding crowd. It was actually my and

Del's spot. And it would be again once we were reunited as partners. Sorry, kid.

"Castley."

"Castley Cresswell." He leaned back against the wall and spoke to the ceiling. "What a name. I know your little sister. What's her name, Baby J? That's a weird-ass name. No offense. That's not her real name, is it? I mean, I hope it's not on her birth certificate. Oh, shit." He sat up, eyes wide. "You're not allowed to talk to me, are you?"

"I just told you my name is Castley."

"Oh yeah." He sat back again. "Duh. You know what? That's a great name. I bet you a ton of girls would love to have it."

"They're welcome to it."

"Ha. Hey. Do you know what my name is? George. Gray, not that it matters." He wiped his nose. He had a kind of dreamy look, all rubbery and loose. His spiky hair was practically landscaped. "I used to think George was kind of a dope name, because you had the monkey and everything. Curious. But now there's Prince George. And that kind of ruins it, in a way." He frowned like he was lost. He wasn't the only one. I hoped that he would stay lost, but he managed to pick up his train of thought, if you could call it that. "Oh yeah, but back to my original point, we both kind of have royal names. You, Castley. And me, Prince George. Or even King George."

"How was that your original point?" I asked, but the bell rang, saving me from one of his twisted trains of thought.

Delvive and I went to Admin during first break and confirmed exactly what we'd suspected. The only way for us to be in the same drama class was for me to take a math class other than CPM 3. Delvive couldn't swap out of Calculus because that was the highest math Almsrand offered—she couldn't go backward. I didn't have to take Calculus; the counselor brightly informed me that I could just take Algebra 2 first period. I could also poke out my own eyes with a stick.

Neither of us really knew what to do. Strike that— Delvive knew what I needed to do, and she patiently waited for me to make the right decision.

"I have Drama right now," she said. "I really need you to switch, Cass. I'll help you with Algebra 2. I'll even do all your homework."

"And will you take all my tests?"

She shook my arm. "Why not? We look alike. No one at this school can tell the difference anyway."

She did have a point, but it wouldn't be that easy. "What if we both have a test on the same day? What if you get sick?"

She held her book bag tight against her side. "Castley, if he finds out—"

"He won't. Just make sure you pick a girl partner— don't let Mrs. Fein pick for you." I didn't mention that my own partner was of the male species. Because no one would ever find out. Not Father, not anyone. That was the clearest road to happiness.

Delvive ended up partnering with Emily Higgins. Emily was a staunch born-again, so I thought Del would at least be comfortable, but she stopped talking to me, except to say, "I won't tell. But if he already knows, I'm resting the blame squarely on you."

There was a latent belief in our family that Father just knew things. And sometimes he did. Sometimes the things he said or the things he predicted were exactly right. Like with Hannan. He knew Hannan was going to be a football player. I mean, he said "Hannan is going to be the high school quarterback" when Hannan was only seven or eight.

Some people would say that Hannan became the quarterback *because* Father said that, that Father gave him permission and put the idea in his head. But the Almsrand High School football team was one of the best in the state. It wasn't the sort of team you could get onto just by wanting to. And when Hannan first started playing football, he was good, but he certainly wasn't amazing, and the other boys used to make fun of him because he was a Cresswell. But over time, he got better, and the other players grew to respect him, and then, like magic, Hannan became the high school quarterback.

Thinking about it scared me. It really did. Because I couldn't tell the difference, I really didn't know, when Father was right and when he was wrong.

Instead of going straight to the house after school, I went to see Mortimer. I should've gone straight home to avoid getting in trouble, but Caspar agreed that it was a nice idea, so I went.

As I descended the steps leading down into the amphitheater, knots formed in my stomach. Caspar may have been forgiving, but Mortimer was going to be pissed off.

But it's not your fault, I reminded myself. *Mortimer's the one who stole from the shop. Mortimer's the one who got caught.* Although it had been my idea.

The amphitheater was a great stone edifice dating

back hundreds of years. It was once used for religious revivals, but it had been abandoned by time and distance. There was a wide stage with a great black mark burned into the center, where they must have lit fires in the olden days, and there was a stone wall behind it, with towers and turrets and bare flagpoles.

I walked around the back of the stage, aware that Morty would hear me coming. I peered through the grate, but I didn't see anything but shadows.

"Morty?"

"Fuck off." His voice came up from below, dry with disuse.

I sighed and dropped my book bag. "I'm *sooorry*."

"Actually fuck off."

I kicked the dirt. "Mortimer. I'm serious. I just came down here to say sorry, okay? I don't know what I was thinking."

"You swore on Momma's life."

Had I? I tried to think back. "No. That was about the cold sore. I didn't say anything about the cold sore."

"You fucking said *antiviral cream*!"

"Stop swearing."

"Can you just go? Please, darling sister."

"I could let you out."

64

He appeared, suddenly, behind the grate. His fingers curled around the bars. "Are you seriously leading me astray again?" He cocked his eyebrow.

"Not now, maybe," I said, scanning the trees. "But after dark. So you don't have to spend the night down there."

I could see him debating. It was a tempting offer. It had to be horrible down in that cave when darkness fell and seemed to stretch on and on forever. I had never been down there, not even for a peek. I was too afraid. Afraid the door might shut above me. Afraid of the click of the lock.

"Unless, of course, you have other plans," I said. I was thinking specifically of Lisa Perez coming to kiss him in the dark, but my heart wouldn't let me say it. It thumped in my chest, so loud it drowned my thoughts.

"Come back tonight and I'll give you my answer." His fingers slid from the bars and he vanished into the dark.

Caspar would definitely not approve of my plan, so I was careful to avoid his penetrating gaze all through the afternoon and into the night. We spent the afternoon "cleaning out" the yard, which involved both cleaning and fixing up things to sell. Father was going to the market that weekend, so he needed anything and everything that would fetch a price.

I was clearing out a dresser we'd dragged from one of the storage rooms downstairs. The drawers were filled with wires, tangled into one big heap. Father didn't believe in wires, so I was cutting them apart with scissors and throwing them away.

Inside one drawer, there were so many wires, I thought I might keep pulling forever and never reach the end. Del noticed my struggle and walked toward me. The wires came free with a jerk, and I saw something underneath. By "something" I mean a photograph, of three people and a baby.

"Need help?" Del said.

I opened my mouth to speak, then stopped. I recognized something in the photo. Not a person, not exactly, not right off the bat, but I recognized something telling me to be quiet, and I stuffed the photo into the pocket of my dress.

"What was that?" My siblings seriously noticed everything.

"It's pornographic," I said so she wouldn't ask to see it. Del made a face. "I'll get rid of it."

"You do that."

We had dinner—tinned food and bread Father made because Momma's hands were too bad. It was always dry and doughy at the same time, but it cured hunger because after you ate it, you never wanted to eat again.

I felt the picture in my pocket all through dinner, like it actually was pornographic. I wanted to look closely at it, but I couldn't do that anywhere in the house without being detected. I would have to wait until I was alone, which, with five siblings, might never happen.

After dinner we all gathered in the family room to read scriptures. We each read from our own book. Jerusalem's was the prettiest, but also the scariest, because she drew pictures every so often. Pictures of planets circling each other in phantom orbits, of monsters that preyed on the weak-willed with their wild eyes and razor-sharp teeth, of locked boxes with no keys. My book was the messiest, which used to bother me, but didn't anymore.

We all took our places around the room, less Mortimer, and read a verse. We always read until bedtime, although sometimes we read on much later, usually when something was troubling Father. We would just read and read and read like the words were supposed to take us somewhere.

That night Father stood by the window, staring out onto the road like he expected visitors. He was distracted, so we all were.

Del sighed. " 'And when the cloud descends it brings The End and when The End comes: clarity. The mind is sharpened on the point of a knife.' "

Hannan continued, " 'God has called you as a prophet. You will see things as they are, beyond the veil of humanity. You are the child of his visions. You are the—' "

"What does that mean?" Father looked up, as if he genuinely didn't know.

Hannan shifted. "It means he's a prophet?" Genius.

"Who is?"

"Um . . ." Hannan looked down at his book. "The person this book is about."

"And who is this book about?"

"Um." Hannan scratched his neck. "You?"

"God," Father corrected. "This book is about God."

Hannan cocked his head. "So God called himself as a prophet?" The sad thing was, he probably didn't realize this made no sense.

"No. The book is about God and his prophet, but the prophet and God are one and the same."

Hannan nodded. "Interesting." Kill me now.

The thing about Father's book was, it only made sense when I didn't think about it. Most of the time, if I tried to disassemble it, if I tried to look at it logically, I hit a wall. But other times I read something, found something, like buried treasure, that made me realize that God, and maybe even my father, knew the exact shape of my heart.

"Castella, continue please."

" 'You will hide your true self. You will bury what you fear, in a locked chest in the cave of your heart, where you will keep the bones of the person you could have been.' "

We finished scriptures at eight o'clock. I wanted to take a quick bath and then sleep for a few hours before I went to get Mortimer, but Hannan got into the bathroom first. Hannan could spend actual hours in the bath, so I surrendered immediately and went to my room.

On the way down the hall, I passed by Father's old room. There was a light patch on the floor where the bed used to be. When we were really little, we all used to crowd on the bed together, me and Caspar and Hannan and Delvive and Mortimer and Jerusalem, and listen to Father tell stories while Momma beamed at him like he'd invented happiness.

I hovered in the doorway. It was funny how pretty the past could be, prettier than the present, safer than the future because you knew what happened. All you had to do was interpret it, tell yourself a story, and it could be as pretty or as horrible as you wanted it to be.

I looked away and continued on to my bedroom.

Jerusalem was painting next to the window. Sometimes she would stay there well into the dark, painting by moonlight. She was obsessed with paintings of the universe—big, bold depictions of planets and stars and moons. She didn't even draw in pencil first. She just painted onto the canvas with a kind of relaxed serenity, like she had all that and more in her little finger.

Right then she was painting a picture of two planets colliding—little pieces were flying everywhere—but it looked oddly pleasant, almost like they were embracing.

Del was on her mattress with an enormous book on her lap.

"Can we turn the lights out?" I collapsed on my mattress. "I feel kind of sick."

Del's eyes bounced up. "So I suppose that means you're not going anywhere tonight?"

"I have no immediate plans."

"Don't you think that's a bad idea?"

"I said, *I don't have any immediate plans.*" Del liked to think she could read my mind; it was the triplet factor. Luckily for me, it was also complete bull.

She looked back down at her book. "I need the lights on. I have homework."

"What homework do you have on the first day of school?"

"Calculus." It would have to be Calculus.

I groaned and pushed myself off my mattress.

"Where are you going?"

Jerusalem's brush froze midstroke.

"I'm going to sleep out in the woods, where they don't have any Calculus."

"Castley!" Del looked to Jerusalem for support, but she went back to painting. Del sighed and rubbed her temple. "Just try not to get caught this time. Please."

I tapped my fingers along the door frame. "I love you, too."

The moment I crossed the tree line, I reached into my pocket and brushed the photograph. Once I was far enough to feel safe, I stepped into the light of the moon and took it out of my pocket. It was a picture of three normal teenagers and a very small baby. Three teenagers, and one of them was definitely my father; you couldn't mistake him anywhere. He had the same crazy light in his eyes, only on a young face it looked purely magical, charismatic even. He was wearing a jersey with the number seven (it had to be seven), and beside him was Momma. Momma was beautiful, in a way that was painful to see. Painful, maybe, because of the way that beauty had died. I couldn't place the other boy in the photo, but he was the one holding the baby, which must have been his job as the less pretty one. Father was the only one looking at the camera lens, glaring no less, like even his former self could see what I was doing and was displeased by it.

Looking at the photo was like looking into an alternate universe. And the weird thing was that it didn't just make the past seem different; it made the present feel different as well, like I might actually be someone else, like I might not be who I thought I was, because this photo existed.

I had never, ever considered that Father was once a teenager. Maybe, possibly, even a baby. And he didn't look religious, if someone could look religious. He looked like someone who would have been cast as the lead in the school play. He looked like someone who could have had any life he wanted. So why had he chosen this one?

*   *   *

The woods were insane in the dark, terrifying and magical at the same time. But best of all were the stars, which trumpeted their light into the misty dark.

I tromped along through the forest, crackling leaves and humming happily to myself. I loved the dark because it meant I could be invisible without it hurting so much.

When I reached the amphitheater, I made a hooting sound that reverberated inside the stands.

"Took you long enough!" Mortimer shouted. I bounded down the steps, into the belly of the beast. There was something freeing about the night. It was easy to get carried away.

"What are you talking about?" I skidded to a stop above the trapdoor. I heard the dirt shifting below as he climbed the chute leading into the Grave. "It's still early. I was going to wait a few hours, but Del was driving me crazy, doing her *Calculus*." I dropped down and spun the combination (the number seven, three times). We all knew the combination because sometimes Father would send one of us out to collect whoever was down there (Father insisted the door was locked at all times, even when Caspar was down there).

The lock clicked, and I wrested the door open. Mortimer popped up so fast that I lost my balance.

"Jeez! You scared me!" I whacked his shoulder.

He took me in his arms and ran me backward so we fell against the stone steps. "Thank you, thank you, thank you! Thank you for rescuing me." He kissed my neck.

"Oh my God, do not give me neck herpes!" I shoved him off of me. His eyes were shining. "What are we going to do?"

"I don't know," he said, zipping up his hoodie like he had a plan. "Maybe we should go for a stroll downtown."

Normally, I wouldn't agree to such a thing. Especially not so early, when there would definitely be people around. But all that stuff with Lisa Perez and drama class was making me feel rebellious. Or was it just hopeful?

"Okay," I said. "Let's go."

Mortimer raised his eyebrows. He'd expected me to say no. He may have been kidding, or testing me. But he didn't back down. He reached out and took my hand and dragged me toward the highway.

Father knew exactly what he was doing when he paired me off with Caspar. Mortimer and I together were a very bad idea.

The outskirts of Almsrand were all farms and trailer parks, but just past the high school there was a ribbon of traffic lights and chain restaurants that could have been Any Place, USA. We could see the strip lights up ahead. The entire town was trapped in a white box of light, like a stage in a darkened theater.

We pulled to a stop in the thick brush at the edge of the woods.

"I don't think you should wear that." Mortimer nodded at my dress. We made our own dresses, Delvive, Jerusalem, and I, because Father couldn't find clothes shapeless enough. Instead he brought us faded materials that we sewed into box-shaped dresses. We weren't exactly seamstresses, either, so we tended to leave hems unfinished, shoulders uneven. "Everyone's gonna know you're one of us."

"Yeah, because you really blend with your electric-blond hair," I noted. He popped his hood up. "Mortimer! Where are you?" I put my hands out, searching the air for him.

He whacked my hands away. "Shut up."

I laughed. "I don't know what you expect me to do. Strip off my dress and walk around naked? Would that make me blend?"

He thought for a second. "I'll take off my shirt and you can wear that."

"Without pants?"

"It's long enough. Girls do it all the time."

"That was, like, early 2000."

"I hate to break it to you, Cass, but what you're wearing is, like, early 1800."

"Fine." I held my hand out.

He unzipped his hoodie and turned around to take off his shirt. He didn't want me to see his collarbone. I remembered the day he broke it, even though I tried not to think about it. Father had gone to collect Mortimer in the Grave. I had been upstairs in my room, writing lame poetry in my notebook, when I heard them coming up through the woods. Heard them because Mortimer wouldn't stop screaming.

Mortimer had always been the disobedient one, so at first everyone thought he was just trying to get attention. Slowly, we all gathered downstairs, drawn by the screams. Father stood in the corner of the room, face pale and bewitched. He told Mortimer to stop in a weak, distracted way. But Mortimer kept on howling, with his hand braced over his heart, and then he sat down hard on the floor. Caspar got down on the floor to comfort him. He tried to calm him, tried to quiet him. He unbuttoned his shirt, to give him air, and he said, "I think his—" and then he stopped, and he fell back on his butt. Because Mortimer's collarbone was poking out of his skin.

When we did finally go to the hospital, the doctor said that usually collarbones healed themselves, so maybe it wasn't so bad that Father had tried to push the bone back in. That Father insisted it would heal itself in God's time. Mortimer never would have gone to the hospital if Michael Endecott hadn't showed up at our house, just out of the blue (Father said he spied on us). He heard Mortimer screaming, and when he saw him, he got into a huge fight with Father. Then Michael Endecott pretty much kidnapped Mortimer and took him to the hospital.

That was when the state separated us, when they tore our house apart, forced us into a real school. Those were the worst days of my life. But Mortimer told the police it was an accident, even though Michael Endecott (who couldn't have known anyway) continued to insist that it wasn't, that there was something wrong with our father and our house, that we were being "abused."

I thought about the word sometimes. Mainly when I was worried that other people were thinking it. Because I didn't feel abused. Only I didn't know. I didn't know what abuse felt like because I didn't know whether I was experiencing it or not. And anyway, wasn't it just something someone told you? Wasn't it just another thing you believed? And if I believed that everything was okay and if Mortimer believed it was an accident, then wasn't that what it was?

"Here," he said, tossing his shirt over his shoulder. I hid behind a bush to change, lifting my dress up over my head and feeling the cool night air blowing against my old-fashioned underwear.

"I don't know if it's going to be long enough to cover my shorts." We girls all wore long cotton shorts that went down past our knees.

"Take those off, too," he said with a snort.

"You're disgusting."

"Girls do it, you know. Modern girls do it."

"This one doesn't." I rolled up the shirt's sleeves and stepped out from behind the bush.

Mortimer fake-ogled. "Wow. You almost look like a normal person."

"You look like an anemic rat."

"Be more creative."

"What should we do with this?" I held up my dress.

"I suppose burning it is not an option?"

"Got a light?" I teased. A flint snapped. Mortimer held up a gold-colored Zippo lighter.

"Where did you get that?"

"I found it." He waved it from side to side, causing the flame to flicker. "Do you really want to torch the sucker or what?"

"Seeing as I have, like, three dresses, I'll keep this one."

"All right. Don't say I didn't give you the option. Hide it under a bush or something."

It was weird to see my bare legs as I crouched down to hide my dress. It was a good thing I had fair hair, because you couldn't really tell I'd never shaved in my life. With my industrial black boots and my pale, scrawny legs, I almost looked cool.

"Let's go," I said, genuinely smiling for, maybe, the first time in my life.

six

When the first person passed us on the normal street in the normal town, I grabbed Mortimer's hand. He let me. We walked that way for a while, stopping occasionally to gaze into darkened shop windows as if we were shopping after hours, when really all we wanted to do was look at ourselves—him all Goth in his hooded sweater and me, bare-legged, grunge—and imagine what it would be like if we were normal kids from a normal family.

"Everything would be different, wouldn't it?" I gushed. "If we were like everybody else. What do you think Caspar would be like?"

Mortimer rolled his eyes. "Caspar's probably the only one of us who would be exactly the same."

I squeezed his hand. I knew I should let go, but I couldn't. What if I got lost, sucked away, by this real and different world?

We walked up and down Main Street for about half an hour before Mortimer started to get bored. He wanted to take it to the next level, the way he always did.

"Let's go sit in a restaurant," he said, bouncing my hand in his eagerness. "Or a bar or something."

"We're not going to get into a bar." I released his hand. "And we don't have money for a restaurant."

"So what? We'll drink tap water."

"I don't really want to do that." We were across the street from the Pig, a shady dive bar. I could see men smoking in the back garden, their eyes sometimes glowing with refracted light, and it made me think about what Father said, about how Satan was everywhere, in everyone.

"Well, what are we going to do, just keep walking up and down like this?" He threw his arms up in frustration.

I wanted to go home. Needed to go home. *Too late, my friend. You shouldn't have agreed to this.*

Mortimer stuffed his fists in his pockets and jaywalked toward the bar.

"Where are you going?"

"I'm going to ask someone for a cigarette." Mortimer spat in the street.

I jogged after him. Mortimer and I had both smoked before, first when I was about twelve and he was eleven. We'd found a half a pack out in the woods and we decided to try them. It wasn't exactly the time of my life, but I guess it was something to do.

Mortimer let himself into the back garden while I stood by, bouncing from foot to foot. I tried not to look at my legs, which felt more naked than before, but it was hard to avoid them when they glowed like beacons in the dark. A man watched me from his table. He had a waxy face, drooping from his eyes down to his neck.

"Nice ass," he said.

"I beg your pardon?"

"Nice ass," he repeated.

I went cold all over. I had never, ever, in all my life, had a man make a physical comment about my body. I didn't like it. And I knew, in the coldest, surest gasp of certainty, that I was doing wrong. I shouldn't have been out there in the dark, wearing nothing but a goddamn T-shirt and boots like a truck stop hooker.

"Got some." Mortimer passed by, flashing a pair of cigarettes. "Come on, let's go."

I followed him up the road, away from the bar. My shoulders were stiff. I was terrified the man might yell after me, that he might shout so loud that the whole world would hear. *Nice ass.* I wanted to throw up. I felt dirty underneath my skin.

"You okay?" Mortimer said, lighting a cigarette. He held it out to me. "Got you one."

"I don't want it!" I slapped his hand away.

"Okay. Jeez. Chill out." He put the cigarette in his own mouth and let it dangle.

"What are we doing?"

"Huh?"

"I mean, why are we doing this? We know it's wrong."

He exhaled, spewing smoke from his nose. "Give me a break, Cass. Are you seriously gonna pull this one again?" I didn't respond. "You get me into these stupid situations and then you suddenly flip out and, like, change your whole personality."

"I know. I don't know." I covered my face with my hands. "God. I don't know what I'm doing. I wish Caspar were here."

"Are you going to cry or something?" His voice jumped up an octave. "Please don't cry."

"I'm not going to cry," I said through my hands. I let

them drop. "I just feel so confused, you know? Or, like, I do things without thinking and then my brain catches up and it's all messed up."

"Castley." He put his hand on my shoulder. "Seriously. It's not the end of the world."

I gazed at the trees. "I think I want to go home."

"What about what I want to do? Are you just going to lock me back up?"

"No . . . I . . . If you . . ." I tugged at my braid. "Okay, just, you stay out tonight and then I'll meet you at the amphitheater tomorrow morning before school. Just make sure you're back by then."

Mortimer sighed. "Are you sure you don't just want to have a cigarette? Castley, you don't need to think all the time. Sometimes you need to just pretend you're somebody else."

I laughed without meaning to. "But that's what I do all the time." I walked backward, toward the woods. "I'm sorry. I just . . . Maybe I'm tired or something."

He shrugged, tracing a toe through the dirt. "It's okay, you know. I'll be fine on my own. Thanks for letting me out. And Castley?"

"Yeah?"

"Don't have one of your little moral moments when you get home, okay? Just go to bed."

I nodded. "Okay. I promise." I hesitated for a moment, wanting to ask him what he planned on doing, debating whether I should stay after all. Then I took a deep breath and ran back toward the woods.

Once I was safely in the woods, I took my time. I let the night wash over me. I was the night: endless and bodiless and fearless. I stopped to carve a star into the foot of a tree.

This is to remind me how lucky I am. To belong some-where. To be safe.

I drew the five corners: Hannan, Del, Caspar, Morty, and Jerusalem. And me at the center, buried in the heart.

The house didn't look so bad as I approached it. It looked familiar, and that was something. I was about to cross into the yard when I saw Caspar, not two feet away from me, eyes glowing disks in the moonlight.

"Jesus!" I clutched my chest. "What are you doing out here?" He must have gone to see Morty. He must know he was gone. He must realize I had let him out.

"What are *you* doing out here?" It was weird to hear Caspar answer my question with a question. His eyes were wide and his shoulders were tense, like I'd caught him doing something he shouldn't. But hadn't *he* caught *me*?

"Nothing." I tried to shrug. "Couldn't sleep."

"Same," he said, too fast. I looked at him, and he looked at me, and we both knew the other was lying. "Do you want to go first?"

I opened my mouth to tell him everything, but he gestured toward the yard. "Oh. Okay. Good night."

"Night."

I actually slept well that night for the first time in a long time. I guess I was tired, but I think I was also satisfied. Sometimes you had to test yourself to figure out what you really wanted, and after trying to be a "normal girl" for a while, I knew that was definitely not what I wanted. And I felt happy and lucky, right up until I saw Mortimer the next morning.

When I told Caspar I was going to see Mortimer again on the way to school, I had a hard time convincing him not to come with me. I knew that Caspar was a forgiving person, and if he found out that I'd let Mortimer out, he wouldn't scold me and he wouldn't tell Father. But I was worried he would look down on me just the same.

"I really think I should go see him," he insisted, pouty lips all screwed up as we pushed through the forest.

"No." I sighed. "I don't want to hurt your feelings or anything, but he asked me to ask you not to come." It was a lie, but I knew Mortimer would understand. It had to be done. It was easier that way.

"But why wouldn't he want me to see him?"

"I think . . . maybe he's embarrassed or something."

"But he shouldn't be embarrassed. Why would he be embarrassed?"

"Well, he did kiss Lisa Perez." I thought maybe I could scare Caspar off if I started talking about sexy stuff. Trouble was, I wasn't exactly comfortable with it myself.

"That's nothing to be ashamed of."

"Yeah, but, um, he . . ." I had no idea what to say.

"Castley, I'm sure it's fine," he said, altering his course so he was heading toward the amphitheater.

"But he said you make him feel bad!"

He froze. "What?"

"I don't know." I snapped a twig with my fingers so it dropped limp in my hands. "Because everything you do is always so *perfect*. Sometimes it's kind of hard to take."

He turned away from me. His face was pointed at the ground, but I still saw enough to know I had wounded him. And the worst part was, I think he knew that I wasn't talking about how Mortimer felt. I think he knew that I was kind of, sort of, talking about how I felt.

When I reached the Grave I called out carefully, quieted by the sun lifting into the sky. "Morty? Are you here?" I moved toward the sewer grate, but saw only the dark.

"Where did you put my shirt?" His voice sounded rumpled.

"Oh." I had it folded at the bottom of my book bag. I sat down to dig it out.

"Can you hurry up? I'm freezing."

"Don't you have your sweatshirt?" He didn't reply. He didn't appear behind the grate.

I piled my CPM book and my notebooks on the ground and took out his T-shirt. "Here." I held it up to the grate. He didn't reach out to get it. "Mortimer, *here*."

"Just leave it there."

I felt a chill—*bzzt*—sting my heart. "What do you mean? Why?" I slid closer, dragging my dress through the dirt. "Why won't you let me see you? What happened?"

I peered into the murky dark of the cave. He stood suddenly, and the skin of his bare chest flashed in the light.

It was obvious he'd tried to wash himself. There were

fingerprints in the black ash that streaked his body. His skin was bright pink in places. The pinkness caught in the light so it burned.

"Oh my God. What happened?"

"Don't say, Oh my *you-know-what*." He snatched his shirt out of my hands.

"Mortimer. What happened? What did you do?" I wasn't sure if I was imagining it, but I thought I smelled smoke. I thought of the Zippo. Maybe the cigarette had burned him. Maybe God had punished him for smoking by making him catch fire. "What happened to your sweat-shirt?"

He just laughed, slipping on his T-shirt.

"You better do something about that—whatever that black stuff is."

"Ash."

"Mortimer. What did you do?"

"Nothing, dear sister. Nothing you should worry about. Now, lock me up and get to school."

"Morty." I wrapped my fingers around the bars, but he dropped down into the shadows.

I would be late for school if I didn't hurry. And maybe it was better, better if I stayed away from Mortimer for a while. Because trouble seemed to follow him the

89

way he followed trouble. It was like they were chasing each other's tails and one day they would swallow each other up.

All day at school my ears were perked, listening for any hint of a fire, but I didn't hear a thing. Although, to be fair, I didn't really talk to anyone, except for George Gray, who talked *at* me as usual. He told me that his parents were getting a divorce because his father cheated and his mom wouldn't put out (I wish I were kidding). He also told me he was on the freshman football team and that Hannan was the best football player he had ever seen in his entire life.

Caspar didn't speak to me at lunch. I think he was truly mad at me.

But I needed to talk to him. I really needed to tell him about Mortimer. Because as the day wore on, I became more and more convinced that Morty had done something horrible. And if he had, then wasn't it also sort of my fault? Because I had helped him do it. I had let him out.

What if he'd started a wildfire? Or burned down the church altar? Or sacrificed a goat? And no one would ever know it was him, no one would know because he had an alibi, an ironclad alibi. *I was locked in a cave in the middle of the woods.*

I felt completely paranoid. I was sure that the police or Father would come storming through the classroom doors. *I told you God was watching! Did you really think you could help Mortimer escape from God's Chambers and there wouldn't be consequences?*

After school I felt so sick that instead of helping with the junk sale, I went upstairs and lay down on my mattress alone. Sunlight streamed down through the window on my pale, sad body, and I moped and wallowed in a fear that came from no direction.

After a while, I heard footsteps on the stairs. I squeezed my fists together, hoping it was Caspar. It was Father.

He stood in the doorway. "Are you all right, Castella? Hannan said you are sick. What's the matter?"

"I'm fine, I think. I just feel bad."

He came into my room and sat down on the floor beside me. When Father sat down, he looked impossibly young. He was slim and compact, like a dancer. When he sat down he didn't look intimidating. When he sat down he looked a lot like Caspar.

"What do you feel bad about, darling?" He brushed my cheek with his thumb.

"I don't know. Everything. Like, just the whole world, maybe."

"Of course you do," he said, and for a moment I felt right with it, with myself. He brushed my hair back and spoke in his magical voice. "The world is a terrible place. And people like us don't belong in it. That's why we feel so uncomfortable here. Because we're not meant for this world, you see? We're different. We're special. You are especially, Castella." He took a deep breath. "I know it is difficult, but this is only a waiting period. Keep your eyes fixed firmly on heaven. That is where we belong. You and Caspar, Hannan and Delvive, Jerusalem and Mortimer. We'll all be happy there. We'll be at peace. For this turmoil you feel is but a symptom of mortal flesh, nothing more. And if you think hard, if you focus your mind, you will see that this world isn't real. This world doesn't even exist. Only heaven does."

Some of the things Father said made me feel better. Some of the things he said felt right. And right then, I wanted to be in heaven, with Caspar and everyone else. Right then, it didn't seem like such a bad option after all.

Father let Mortimer out on Wednesday afternoon. All evening I felt nervous, sure that someone would notice the burns hidden up his sleeves or the fact that his favorite hoodie had disappeared. It wasn't that I wanted him to be punished, but when he wasn't, I felt uneasy.

Things didn't really get better from there. Del still wouldn't talk to me. Jerusalem still wouldn't talk to anyone. And I was pretty sure Caspar was ignoring me, although he did it so politely that I couldn't tell if it was real or if I was just imagining it—which made me a little suspicious about Caspar generally. Perhaps he wasn't as naive as I'd always thought.

I spent the rest of the week alone. I didn't talk to anyone. The only person who talked to me was George Gray. Because I was so desperately lonely, I didn't find him as annoying as I had at first. I found comfort in Drama, in playing pretend. It was the only time and place where I didn't feel afraid, because I could truly imagine I was someone else. It was the only time I didn't have to worry about the truth, because everything was supposed to be a lie.

George actually wasn't a bad actor, although there was a certain degree of bravado that accompanied every part he played. Mrs. Fein started us off doing cold readings and playing games that were supposed to bond us as scene partners. None of this stuff was graded, so most people didn't do it; they just spent the hour gossiping or involved in drama class intrigues. Even Del and I hadn't bothered most of the time, but George took it all very seriously, with the kind of enthusiasm especially reserved for people of the freshman persuasion.

"You should use your body more when you act," he told me. I gave him a look. "No, I mean, you're really stiff. Your voice is good, but, I mean, I can kind of tell you're not letting go completely."

The only thing worse than criticism was criticism that was right.

I took a deep breath. I moved my body in a wave. "How's this?"

He tilted his head. "I can't really see what you're doing under those clothes."

I put my hands on my hips. "First I'm not moving my body enough; now you want me to take off my clothes?" This was why Father didn't want me to have a male drama partner.

He smiled, then grew serious. He put his hand on my shoulder. It was an intense moment. "You're supposed to let go; that's the whole point of drama. You're supposed to, like, completely lose yourself."

My breath caught. "What if you don't have a self to lose?"

"Then it should be easier, I guess."

We Cresswells sat together every lunch hour to demonstrate that, yes, we were freaks, but we practiced containment. That afternoon Mortimer had to stay behind, so I sat next to Caspar to test whether he was ignoring me. He moved to make space for Jerusalem, either to get away from me or because he knew Jerusalem didn't like to sit on the outside. Or both.

"How is everyone's day going?" I asked. No one answered. We didn't really talk to anyone at school unless it was required, and we weren't required to talk to one another. Everyone ate his or her food in silence, and I realized I'd better hop to before Hannan asked if he could have mine.

I was doing just that when she appeared. We were so unaccustomed to people appearing that she probably stood there for ages before anyone noticed her. And when I finally did, I had no idea who she was there for. *She* was the girl from the Great American, the girl from the truck. The Michael Endecott girl.

She was fiercely pretty, but also just fierce. We all

scanned one another's faces, questioning, and not in a nice way—in a furtive, accusatory way. Someone was in trouble.

The girl seemed to agree, because she opened her mouth and said, "Which one of you was it?"

No one said anything for long enough to establish that was the way we operated.

She shook her head. Put her hands on her hips. She seemed to think this would be a big concern with us. *Which one of you was it?* She didn't know us well enough to realize that we cared as much about other people as other people cared about us.

Except Caspar. He was really uncomfortable. I don't think he could stand not answering a question. She could probably tell, because she glared especially at him. Then she said, almost hesitantly, "Was it you?"

He stood so abruptly that we all moved sideways, as if forced by a wave. Hannan raised his eyebrows. We all waited for Caspar's explanation.

He wrung his lips and opened his mouth. "I promised Miss Syrup I'd help her set up the classroom," he said. "Come with me?"

The girl seemed weirded out. She was trying to figure out which one it was who had done something that seemingly upset her, and now she was being asked to volunteer for charity. Welcome to Caspar.

"Um . . . okay?" she said. They went. I sat back and looked at my brother and sisters, who were eating their lunches like nothing had happened.

"What was that all about?" I said.

Hannan shrugged. "Caspar was just trying to deflect the situation. Classic defense technique." Thank you for the sports analysis.

"No, I mean, what she said: 'Which one of you was it?' "

Hannan chewed thoughtfully for a second. Then he said, "Mortimer." And even I had to admit he was probably right.

On Saturday morning, Caspar and Jerusalem went to the market with Father, but they came back early. Father said the market was deserted and that next week they'd have to try Huxley, which was farther away but usually busier.

I caught Caspar and Mortimer heading out to the lake that afternoon, and even though neither of them wanted me there, I tagged along behind them.

Once we reached the lakeshore, I tried to cozy up to Caspar to get him to forgive me. "So, how's school?"

"Fine." He was watching Mortimer undress with a strange expression on his face.

I glanced over and my heart dropped. As Morty unfastened his buttons, the burns on his skin flashed pink. They were sprayed across his body like paint. He removed his shirt. His right arm was the worst, snug in a swollen pink sleeve of burnt flesh.

Caspar stiffened. "What happened to your arm?"

Morty lifted his wrist, observing it with disinterest. "It got burnt."

Caspar's right eye twitched. He jerked forward, then stopped himself. I could almost see something burning then, up from his toes and all through him. I felt it in the air. I had never seen Caspar angry in my entire life. It produced a strange sensation in the pit of my stomach.

"Caspar?" I said.

"Oh, really?" He coughed. "When was that?" His eyes flashed in my direction.

"Why are you looking at *me*?"

Morty shrugged slowly. "Gosh. I don't really remember. . . . But I think maybe you do," he sneered at Caspar.

I put my hands up. "I have no idea what either of you are talking about. Just in case that isn't clear by my blank expression."

"You . . . Why would you do that?" Caspar asked.

"Why would you do *that*?" Mortimer shot back.

"See, I still don't really know what you two are talking about." Both sets of eyes were on me. Keeping quiet time.

Caspar kicked the sand with his toe. "I just wanted to make sure that she was okay."

"Okay?" Mortimer laughed. "Okay when she ratted me out to that freak of nature? Do you know how much trouble she could have got me in? I mean, if it weren't for this one blowing it first." He motioned to me.

"Who are you talking about? Who did you want to make sure was okay?"

"What were you doing with her, anyway?" Mortimer pressed. "I mean, you certainly took your time making sure she was *okay*. Were you giving her a *full body checkup*? Were you making sure she was all right *inside and out*?"

"Mortimer." Caspar's voice was steely. "Don't say things like that."

"Or what? *Or what?* Are you gonna hit me, Caspar?" He whacked his bare chest. He was at least a foot shorter than Caspar, but I didn't doubt he could get a few shots in, especially since Caspar would probably have to pause between punches to ask for forgiveness. "Come on, let's see what you got."

"I don't . . ." Caspar shook his head to clear it. "I don't understand why you're being like this."

"People change. You have."

"You're completely overreacting."

"You disappoint me. You disappointed me."

Quiet descended, seeming to push everyone farther apart. A bird called in the distance, failing to fill the empty space. I had never, ever seen Caspar and Mortimer argue like that. I didn't understand what they were arguing about. If I didn't know any better, I would swear Mortimer was jealous.

"Maybe we should just go back," I said, spreading my hands wide to herd them together. "Prayers are soon, anyway. It's your day, Caspar."

"I know what day it is, Cass," Caspar snapped.

"We still have two hours," Mortimer said. "Why the hell would we go back now?" At least I had managed to unite them against me.

"Well, what do you want to do?"

Caspar moved suddenly, making me flinch. He stalked toward the woods.

"Wait. Where are you going?" I said.

"Ask Mortimer!"

Mortimer jogged up the beach, shouting behind him.

"That's right! Go tell her about this, too! Tell her *everything*! You traitor! You're a traitor! I hate that man, you tell her that, too! If he ever tries to 'help' me again, I'll kill him!"

Sometimes I hated having brothers. I stayed at the lake with Mortimer. I didn't know what else to do. I had an idea who he was talking about (Michael Endecott), and then there was this *she*. The girl in the truck that day? The one I saw at the Great American? But what did she have to do with Michael Endecott?

I wanted to ask Mortimer about it, but I knew I had to be careful. He wasn't exactly in the best mood.

He was floating in the water, with his swollen arm bobbing beside him.

"Doesn't it hurt?" I said, nodding at it. "When you get it wet?"

"Cold water is good for burns." He lifted his head up. "You know I can still feel it burning sometimes? Under my skin, like it's still on fire."

"That's . . . nice?"

He rolled his eyes at me. "It's like what the book says, about being baptized by fire, how you can still feel it burning."

My nose crinkled. I had never heard Mortimer talk about Father's book that way, like it was something to be admired.

"About the fire . . ." I said, hoping he might keep talking.

He dropped his head back so his ears were surrounded by water. "I don't want to talk about it anymore."

"Are you really mad at Caspar?" I said, but he pretended not to hear me. Sometimes I really hated having brothers.

Caspar was late for prayers, only he didn't get in trouble. He taught his lesson, something about fate and how God worked in mysterious ways. I wanted to get him alone so I could ask him about the fire, but Father found out first.

seven

On Sunday evening we were all gathered in the living room for scripture study. Only Father wasn't there. We sat in our places and tried not to look at Momma or one another. *If everything is planned beforehand, then what does it mean to be late?*

The front door creaked, then flew open, whacking the wall. Father's footsteps came swiftly up the hall. He came in cradling a black bundle.

He looked at Momma first, which was never a good sign. He crossed to the front of the room and, like a magician, he held the bundle over his head so it unfurled into a charred, black flag.

It was Mortimer's hoodie—or what was left of it. One

of the sleeves had been burnt off, and black gashes, charred and flaky, decorated the front.

The sweatshirt dropped to the floor.

"I found this buried out in the woods. I was praying and God led me to it." Father's eyes went to Mortimer. Mortimer's eyes went to Caspar. "I remember the last time I saw it, and the first time I noticed it missing. And I wonder if someone can help me fill in the blank."

I felt myself vanish. Like my body had disappeared to leave my soul swaying in fear. I felt like fear, the mindless, aimless way it burns and wavers like a flame.

The last time he saw it: when Mortimer went down into the Grave.

The first time he noticed it missing: when Mortimer came out of the Grave.

Can someone help me fill in the blank?

Mortimer's eyes caught mine. I knew he was wishing he'd been nicer to me lately, but I wasn't cruel enough to volunteer myself. And I didn't need to.

"Mortimer. Can you please remove your shirt?" Father kicked the sweatshirt aside.

Mortimer's expression contorted. His hands shivered.

"Stand up. Put your book down. And remove your shirt."

"Father—" Caspar said, rising from his seat.

"Sit down, Caspar Cresswell! I have half a mind to punish you, too."

"Then punish me," Caspar said, slipping as he stood so his book dropped, pages smeared against the floor. "I knew about it and I didn't tell. I purposefully kept it from you."

Father stepped forward. His muscles were coiled tight beneath the skin of his arms. "Caspar, will you help your brother remove his shirt?"

"I don't need help," Mortimer said, ripping open the top button, then continuing down. He sputtered and spat as he spoke, both terrified and exalted by his confession. "I didn't tell you because I didn't want you to be implicated, if there were any repercussions. Caspar found out on his own." There was a weird light in Mortimer's eyes, a hungry kind of eagerness that made them snap in the candlelight.

The burns, which I didn't think he was taking very good care of, seemed to look *worse*. His arm had darkened and shriveled, like the molted skin of a snake. He held his arms out in supplication.

"I lit a fire outside Michael Endecott's door to warn him and his stepdaughter to stay away from us." Stepdaughter? The girl at the Great American was Michael Endecott's stepdaughter? And Mortimer had seen Caspar at her house, although he didn't mention that.

Father didn't smile, but his lips twisted up as though they were holding on to something sweet. I tried to catch Caspar's eye, but he was watching the darkness that gathered outside the window.

It was easy to tell when money was tight, because Father raided the food we stored for the Apocalypse. The next morning we had rice and tinned beans. Father set it carefully on the table, making sure not one grain of rice was spilt, and then went to bleach the dishes. Father was obsessed with Palmer's Bathroom Bleach. He used it on everything—the plates, our clothes, even our wood floors, so the ground was always chalky and splintering under our feet.

Hannan dug into breakfast with alacrity, even though I'd heard that his coach actually fed him before practice every morning. Mortimer watched Father with a hunger that wasn't for food. Caspar wasn't there.

"Where's Caspar?" I asked Father as he scrubbed a pan until it flaked.

"Caspar has gone to God's Chambers."

"But why?"

Father leaned against the counter. "Reflection is good for the mind, Castella. It's not always a means of punishment."

I knew Caspar was punishing himself. I considered visiting him before school, but then I remembered what Mortimer said at the lake and I decided against it. If Caspar wanted to punish himself, then maybe he deserved it.

I was actually starting to look forward to drama class every morning. With Del in a different class, Drama was about the only place in my world where I could escape my almost half a dozen siblings.

The next morning, I was racing down the hill to the theater when someone reached out and grabbed me, stopping me in my tracks. It was Mrs. Tulle.

I wasn't used to being touched, especially not by a stranger, so I took my hand back and backed away.

She held her hands up. "Sorry. I didn't mean to frighten you. I wanted to talk to you about Baby J." She said her name funny, *Bay-bee Jaaay*, as if she were savoring it.

"What about her?"

She seemed surprised to hear me speak. She froze for

about ten seconds before shaking out her head. "It's her paintings."

I felt my chest tighten. Was Baby J in trouble? "What's wrong with them?"

"Nothing. Oh, nothing. They're absolutely *breathtaking*." She waited for my agreement, and when it didn't come, she frowned. "That's exactly what it is. They're spectacular. Genius. So unique."

"I'm not really following you." I didn't mean to sound so steely, but I wasn't exactly comfortable talking to strangers.

"She won't show them to anybody. I mean, not *anybody*. Of course I see them and her classmates see them, but I really think . . . I asked her if she would put them on display, just locally, and she said no—I mean, she didn't *say* no." She smiled like it was funny. "Naturally she didn't say so. But she indicated that she wouldn't show them. And then—well, she took all her paintings out of her cubbyhole, and I don't know where they are. I really hope she hasn't done anything to them."

I felt myself sadden, in a lead wave that sunk down to my toes. I had seen the paintings, stacked in the corner of our bedroom.

"I have to go to class," I said. Mrs. Tulle's face fell and

she started to wither away from me the way they all did, frightened by us Cresswells, by the hopelessness they sensed beyond our graying eyes. I watched her walk away and I felt my heart crack. "I don't think she would destroy them!"

Mrs. Tulle turned, offering a weak smile. "I really hope not. I would hate for something so beautiful to be destroyed."

I felt my chest contract. I started to move. Down the hill, toward the theater. I needed to get to the drama room. Drama was a safe place, a happy place. Until I found out we were doing improv.

I hated improv with a passion. I was ridiculously bad at coming up with stuff on the spot. It made me want to throw up and die at the same time. Delvive was the same, so in the past we'd always "disappeared" during improv days. Mrs. Fein, who wasn't exactly a skilled observer, never noticed.

George Gray, on the other hand, loved doing improv. It was where his real skill lay, apparently. He told me so as Mrs. Fein marched us into the theater. I scanned the auditorium for a way out. Red exit signs glowed from all corners.

"Um, George?" I tried to take his hand. "I think I might be sick."

"Mrs. Fein! Mrs. Fein!" he shouted. I felt a wave of relief. He had actually heard me for once. "We'll go first!"

Mrs. Fein turned the stage lights on, so if I unfocused my eyes, the audience became a weak and clouded blob. *You're going to die,* my brain told me. It was probably a bad sign that death scared me less.

Mrs. Fein wasn't exactly creative when it came to prompts. "Okay. You're husband and wife, and you're having an argument."

"Hi, honey, I'm home!" George called robustly. His voice echoed through the theater. I saw the orchestra pit. It seemed to open up before me, wider and wider, like the void inviting me in. It made me think of Caspar, down in the Grave. Of Jerusalem, hiding her paintings.

I shuddered and forced my eyes upward. The stage lights smeared my eyes.

"Miss Cresswell, you need to participate," Mrs. Fein's voice boomed from the dark.

"My name is Castley." The light feathered in my eyelashes as I looked out over the audience.

"This assignment is graded," her voice droned. "You

need to participate or I'm going to have to give both of you a zero. Miss Cresswell, are you listening?"

"Her name is Castley," George Gray said.

"Start again."

I took a deep breath. George sniffled encouragingly at me. I shut my eyes, but in the darkness I tried to hide myself in, Baby J's paintings rose up, bright and wild, roaring through the darkness like a howl in the night.

You will hide your true self. You will bury what you fear, in a locked chest in the cave of your heart, where you will keep the bones of the person you could have been.

And the planets spun. And the stars shot like warning signals across the fragile sky.

And why shouldn't people see that? Mrs. Tulle said the paintings were beautiful, even if they (maybe) scared her. Why did Baby J have to hide away? Why did we all have to hide away? Why couldn't we show our true selves, dressed in paint or hidden in a pantomime?

When I opened my eyes, things looked different.

"Why did you push me down the stairs?"

"What?"

"My leg." I touched it. I swear I felt it burn. "It hurts. I think my leg is broken." I limped slightly. My body had been taken over by something. It wasn't the truth, but it felt so much like it that I could taste it down the back of my throat.

The house rolled up before me, filling the stage of my mind. The flickering gas lamps, the cold, dark stairwell. The sickly sweet smell of mold and bleach.

"Um . . . Sorry?" A nervous titter of laughter washed over the crowd, but it slipped right through me. There was no crowd. Only me and a pretend that felt stronger than reality. Only the pretend pain throbbing in my real leg.

"You're sorry? I can't walk. I'm going to be in a wheelchair for the rest of my life, and you're sorry?" My voice was ragged. My voice was setting itself free.

"Um . . . I don't think it's broken."

I felt righteous indignation burning inside me as I spun to face him, tripping on my bad leg. "Can't you see the bone?" The audience hissed. I heard breaths collecting, stopping. I felt my pulse speed up.

"Um, I don't see it. Maybe you imagined it."

"Uh-uh!" Mrs. Fein scolded. "You can't deny her story."

"Imagined it?" I cackled. "Maybe I did imagine it. Maybe I imagined everything. That's what I tell myself. When you do these things, these awful, terrible things, I tell myself it must all be in my head! I keep you safe by making myself crazy."

George Gray was stumped. The audience was silent. And then hands began to clap.

"Tremendous!" Mrs. Fein called, more surprised than anything. "Absolutely brilliant!"

I tried to smile. George Gray took my hand and pulled me into a bow, then led me off the stage to sit with the audience.

As we sat down, one of the girls turned to say, "Good job." And another one agreed that it was "cool."

I felt proud if I didn't think too much. I watched the other students take their turns, trying to fake passion or make jokes. But my passion was real. And for once that didn't seem like a bad thing.

I let George Gray walk me to my next class, even though Hannan was in it, too, and might see us. George was quiet for once. He kept shooting me strange looks, like he wasn't sure what he was dealing with.

"Hey." He pulled me into a quiet alcove close to my classroom. His fingers stayed on my arm, and my nerves fizzled and started to burn. I had to take my arm back. I had to step away. "What was all that stuff you said in class?"

"It was just acting." I shrugged.

"But it felt real." He had funny lips—thin and kind of

113

rubbery. Nothing like Mortimer's or Caspar's. Nothing special.

"That's because I'm good."

He looked me up and down as though he were trying to find me inside my clothes. "Okay." He bit his thin lip. I stepped out of the alcove. "Hey, Castley?" I stopped. "I think you're really incredible. I just wanted you to know that because . . ." He took a deep breath. "Because it's a nice thing, and I feel like people don't say nice things enough. They think them, but they don't say them. And they should. I think the world would be a lot better if they did."

I arched my eyebrow. "You know, you could have just stopped with you think I'm incredible. You don't have to say everything that's on your mind."

He thought for a beat. "And you don't have to say nothing that's on yours."

I tried to keep my breath from catching—*one, two, three*—like a trigger.

I tried to think of something stupid to say, something to downplay the way those simple words made me feel, but I couldn't. It was too important and it meant too much to me.

*   *   *

After school I went to see Caspar. I felt a sense of deep unease as I climbed down the steps into the amphitheater. It wasn't like with Mortimer, where I knew he was probably just napping or scheming or up to no good. Caspar was genuinely contrite. He was probably begging for forgiveness over some stupid thing that most people wouldn't even think twice about.

I moved slowly along the dirt. I took deep breaths, ripe with the scent of dying leaves. I saw the grate in front of me, opening up like an orchestra pit. I stopped, squared my shoulders, and slowly turned toward home.

"Castella?" I heard his voice, soft and moody, emanating from the ground. The image of Mortimer and Lisa, the one that had burned itself to the back of my mind, filled my head. It was attached to a heady feeling, painted in oxygen. I breathed it in and clung to myself.

I imagined I had come to rescue Caspar, and then I remembered he had put himself down there. How did you rescue someone from himself?

"I just wanted to check if you were okay."

"I'm fine." I couldn't see him through the grate and I thought he must be down on the ground, on his knees.

Birds chirped, way out away in the sunshine above the trees. I smelled the warm mulch of the fall leaves. I knew I should go home, that I might get in trouble for being late, but for once I didn't care.

I sat down in the dirt. I put my bag down and I put my head on top of it. I shut my eyes. And I heard the bird chirping and I felt the Grave beneath me, warming the earth with its holy spirit. And after a while I fell asleep.

"Castella?" I heard Caspar's voice. I was out on the football field with George Gray. He was always in view but just out of reach. I wanted to talk to him, that was all I wanted to do (*kiss him*), but I couldn't do that because he didn't see me.

I wanted to yell, but my mouth was clamped shut. I scraped my fingers along metal cheeks. And then I saw the fire. It started at the hem of my dress, peeling up the fabric like a curtain as it burned toward my heart.

George, I'm on fire! I'm on fire, George! I was screaming, but I knew my lips weren't moving. I rubbed them with my fingers, trying to pry them open.

I was standing in the bed of a truck. The gears shifted, throwing me forward. It was Father's old red truck and it was driving slowly across the football field. It was the Homecoming game, and the stands were loaded with people drenched in green and blue. They were all there to watch us, because I wasn't alone. All of my brothers and sisters were there with me, and my mother in her wheelchair, rolling back and forth along the truck bed. And I couldn't see Father, but there was a shadowy figure behind the wheel, and I knew that must be him.

The gears bounced and I tried to grab on to something, but my fingers came back burning. The fire. The fire at my feet spread across the bed of the truck. And the whole crowd oohed and aahed.

I could see Michael Endecott and the girl. See Lisa and Riva and Emily Higgins. I spread my lips to scream, but the fire filled my mouth. I could see it burning up my brothers and sisters until they were nothing but dancing flames.

George! George, please! I could see the back of his head, his tall body, as he walked up the stands. He was with his friends. They were getting popcorn. My dress had burned away. The fire swelled around my naked body. The audience began to clap.

"Tremendous! Absolutely brilliant!"

Please! Someone! Please someone help me! Please! My brothers and sisters were gone. Even the shadowy figure had disappeared. All that remained were flames, flames and whatever part of me didn't burn.

"CASTELLA!"

Something sharp struck my side and my eyes flew open. I saw the undersides of the trees first, feathering into the blue dark of the evening sky. I kicked out with my leg.

"Hey!" The metal grate clattered. I had made contact. "Castley? Are you okay?" I rolled over in the dirt. Caspar was standing behind the bars, streaked with ash. I touched it, touched the smear above his lip.

"The fire." I shivered.

"What? Castley, no. It's dirt. It's just dirt." He slipped his hand through the bars and took mine. I knew he was trying to comfort me, but it only made my heart beat harder. "You were dreaming. It was just a dream."

My laughter came out hard. In our family, it was never "just a dream." Dreams took on a super importance. They were a means for God to speak to us. We practically lived our whole lives on the strength of Father's dreams.

I wanted to pull away, but I knew he might take it the wrong way. He was just holding my hand. I didn't have to be afraid of everyone's touch. I took a deep breath.

"You can tell me, if you want." He squeezed tighter. So tight, I thought the breath I couldn't catch might suffocate me.

"I don't think I should."

He shifted in the dirt below, moving closer so his lips were pressed between the bars. "Was it bad?" he said. "I have bad dreams sometimes."

That surprised me. We were supposed to share dreams we thought might be significant, and Caspar had never shared a bad dream with us. I sat back on my hands. "Do you ever wonder what's going to happen to us?"

He didn't say anything for a moment, and in that moment he said more than words, because I knew he did wonder. A lot.

He tried to smile, which was completely wrong for the situation, and I watched it crack and disappear. "We just have to remember that this life is only temporary."

"What worries me," I continued, ignoring his meaningless encouragement, "is that if anything ever went wrong, there's no one who could help us. No one in the whole world. I mean, what if something happened"—I wanted to say "because of Father," but I couldn't trust that one, I couldn't say that—"to Father? What would we do then?"

"We have to trust in God to keep him safe." He rested his forehead against the bars. "Castley, it's no good worrying about all the things that could go wrong. God will never test us beyond our abilities."

I sighed, pretending to find comfort in his words. "Okay." I pulled my hand away.

"Castley." His hand grabbed on to my dress, bunching the fabric into a fist. "I would protect you. I'll protect you, okay?"

"What about everyone else?"

He took a deep breath. "I'll protect everyone else, too. I promise. I'll never let anything happen to you."

I observed the bars. "But what if you're not there?"

"Castley." He released my dress and held his palm out until I took his hand. Then he pulled it close to him and kissed my wrist. "No matter what happens to me, no matter where I am—here or a hundred miles away or dead in heaven—I'll protect you. I'll come back for you. I did before, right?" He was referring to his resurrection, and I felt compelled and confused at the same time.

"Okay."

"Castley." He held my hand against his cheek. "I know it's hard sometimes to believe everything we have to believe. To have faith in a heaven we can't see and a father who maybe isn't . . . p-perfect. But I want you to know that you can always have faith in me."

I almost asked him about Michael Endecott's stepdaughter, which would have ruined the moment. But I didn't ask him, and it ruined the moment anyway.

It was time to start hedging my bets. I couldn't rely on Caspar anymore. I couldn't rely on a brother who swore to protect me while under voluntary lockdown. I couldn't rely on siblings who were more confused than I was.

What if my dream really was a prophecy? What if something bad really was coming? In the dream, George Gray had ignored me when he could have saved me. I needed to befriend him to keep that from happening. I needed a friend, that's all it was. Someone outside my family, just in case. I was only hedging my bets.

"You grew up in Almsrand, right? Where do you live?" I asked George. We were supposed to be picking the scene we would perform at the end of the semester, but Mrs. Fein gave us an obscene amount of time to choose, so no one really bothered until the week before.

George's jaw dropped. He didn't have to make it more awkward than it already was. We were sitting in our spot at the back of the lobby, underneath the drinking fountain. Through the glass doors I could see Tommy Gunn and Bobby Wright smoking cigarettes.

"Um, gosh, I live by the, uh, you know, the chicken

place. I live over it. So my house kind of smells. Like chicken. I used to live on Lavender Road, but my dad sold it because of the divorce."

"Yeah, I know where that is."

"Uh, but where do you live?" He flinched as he sat forward. He had this weird habit of flinching when he got excited, like a robot malfunctioning. "I know you live out in the woods, but I don't know where. How far is it?"

"Um, do you know where the lake is?"

"Which lake?"

"The green one? Kind of small?" He shook his head. "Or the old amphitheater?"

"No. I haven't actually been there. I've heard about it, though."

It bothered me that he wasn't familiar with the landmarks surrounding our house. It made me think that maybe they didn't exist, as crazy as that sounded. Maybe we really did live in a separate dimension. *And no one would ever find us if we all just disappeared.*

"I don't know how to explain it to you." I sighed. "It's, like, about three miles from here. In that direction." I pointed out the tall windows.

"Oh, okay. Cool. Tell me more about this amphitheater thing."

My blood pulsed. The amphitheater was sacred. I wasn't really supposed to talk about it. "I don't know. It's just, like, a stage."

"I heard they used to perform satanic rituals there."

"Who did?"

"I don't know. Satanists? People say that in town. There're all these urban legends about it. About sacrificing babies and stuff like that."

"Are you saying we do stuff like that?" I hooked my hand around the drinking fountain and pulled myself up.

"What? No. Of course not. Duh." He grabbed my wrist. It surprised me so much that I let him pull me down. "I know you're not some kind of freak, Castley. You're just a normal person."

"How do you know that?"

"Because. I know you. You're just like everybody else," he said.

I felt a wave of relief. And I don't know if it was because he said I wasn't a freak or just because I knew someone actually *saw* me. That I wasn't like the lake or the amphitheater. I wasn't an urban legend.

"Don't you get it?" he said. "Other people. They don't know you. I mean, they think they do, but they don't know the real you. That's why they don't see that you're just like us. If they actually talked to you, if they just spent time with you, they would know. If you came and hung out with me and my friends, they'd totally like you. You're cool."

"Really?" I said in spite of myself.

"Yeah. Of course. In fact, you should come hang out with us." He scooted closer to me. "We hang out in The Chicken Shop. You should come down sometime. Seriously, my friends would like you."

I was so excited about the idea of actually having friends that instead of saying no, like I knew I should, I felt my lips move and I felt a new sound come out. I felt myself say, "Yeah. I should."

eight

Although I half suspected I would never go to The Chicken Shop, I was thrilled by the possibility. I imagined myself blending, dressed like a normal teenager. I thought I would be the first person in my family to ever have a normal friend, but I was wrong.

On Wednesday evening, we were all gathered in a circle reading scriptures. Caspar was still out in the Grave—at least we thought he was.

Lately there had been a foul atmosphere inside the house. Half of it was caused by hunger, and all of it was caused by Father. Father didn't have a job, so we were reliant on God to provide. And God didn't always work to a consistent schedule.

For dinner that night we'd had tinned tomatoes and

crackers. My stomach felt wretched, but I reminded myself that Caspar hadn't eaten since Sunday, so I shouldn't complain. I should feel clean and holy, or something.

Del and I were lying flat on our stomachs on the floor, and Mortimer, Jerusalem, and Hannan were crowded on the couch. Momma was in her corner, so pale that the gaslight seemed to glow through her skin like a projector.

We were reading from Father's book, which kind of suited the trippy, starved atmosphere, when we heard footsteps whistling through the field in front of our house. No one said anything, until the door opened.

Father scraped his hair back. "Caspar?"

"Yes, sir." I knew it was Caspar speaking, but it didn't sound like him. His voice was faint. And then we heard him whisper. I sat up, clutching the waxy cover of my book to my chest.

Caspar appeared inside the doorway. He looked pale beneath the dirt that had formed a layer over his skin. His eyes were wide and white with fear. But when he spoke, his voice was calm. "I brought someone home. She was lost in the woods and she wants . . . she needs to use our phone. I thought it was the right thing to do."

Father didn't smile or say that it was okay. He didn't do anything but say, "Bring her in."

Caspar went back into the hallway. I heard him whisper to her. It wasn't until she walked through the door that I realized Caspar had completely lost his mind.

He had brought home Michael Endecott's stepdaughter. She strode in with a smooth easiness, like she was completely comfortable in that dingy, dark room with all of us staring at her like hornets in a nest.

Jealousy surged through me. Not because of the way Caspar watched her, but because I knew that I would never look that way. I would never feel comfortable like that, not here in this house or out in the world or anywhere at all.

Father's book clapped shut. "Good evening, Amity." I squeezed my book between my fingers. He knew who she was. "Did you get lost?" For a wild second, Father's anger seemed to flash through the room, as if it were a physical force. What was Caspar doing? What was Caspar thinking? Surely Father wouldn't touch her. She didn't belong to him. But we did.

"Um . . ." She glanced at Mortimer. "Kind of . . . I guess."

"What a strange coincidence," Mortimer said.

Amity made a face at him. "Just a matter of being in the wrong place at the wrong time, but you wouldn't know anything about that."

Mortimer bristled.

"Would you like to use the telephone?" Father's smile tightened.

"If that's okay. I would really appreciate it, sir." How did she do it? How did she look into Father's eyes and not faint? She didn't even blink. I wondered what Amity would think if she knew the way we lived, if she knew the things we believed. I wondered if Caspar had told her. I wondered if Caspar had told her anything.

Father opened his book and flicked through it with an actor's air. It was what he always did before he broke. He went taut, like he was stepping into a role. He was a good actor, Father. His life was a performance. "No trouble at all, dear. Will you come into my office with me?" Caspar moved to follow her. "Caspar. Stay." The book snapped shut. "Come along, dear."

As soon as Father's office door clicked shut, the room exploded. Mortimer spoke loudest.

"You are such a fucking idiot."

"Caspar, what in the world are you doing?" That was Delvive.

Even Hannan mumbled, "What are you thinking, man?" And Baby J put her face in her hands.

Mortimer bounced off the sofa and paced the floor. "Caspar, have you seriously lost your mind?"

128

"She needed to use the phone," he said weakly. "She lost hers."

Mortimer pulled to a stop in front of him. "Did you not even consider that maybe you should have just *walked her home yourself*?"

Caspar was stricken. I don't think he had even considered that. I don't think he had used his brain at all. "Don't make it a big deal," he said between clenched teeth.

"You're worried about me making it a big deal? You're a fucking idiot, I swear to fuck. Why do you have to go get a hard-on over Michael Endecott's fucking stepdaughter?"

"Mortimer!" Momma hissed. I think we'd all forgotten she was there. She blended into the background so much that it was easy to do. The room fell quiet. We all looked toward the office at the same time.

I tried to keep my thoughts from going berserk. He wouldn't kill her, would he? He wouldn't try to punish her? No, he wouldn't. That was crazy. Father wouldn't do that. Father wouldn't do a thing like that. *Not to a stranger when he had us.*

Mortimer collapsed on the sofa, looking more scared than angry. Caspar hurried to Momma's side and tried to find comfort in comforting her, but even she looked scared. She sat far back in her chair as he stroked her arm and murmured softly in her ear.

The office door peeled open and Father reappeared. Amity strode in behind him.

"Hannan, will you give this lady your seat, please?" Father was stone cold as he took his place at the front of the room. Hannan got off the couch and sat down on the floor with Del and me. "Take a seat, please, Amity."

"Thank you." She stepped over me to get to the couch. Mortimer hissed as she sat down.

Father handed her a book. "His Marvelous Plan, chapter fourteen, verse six."

"It's on page one hundred and thirty-six," Caspar said. His voice took on a disturbing slickness when he addressed her.

"It's one ninety-three in that book," Mortimer snapped.

It was weird to see a stranger in our house, holding our book. Her eyes were bright with curiosity as she fumbled through the thin pages, looking for the verse.

"Castella!" Father yelled. I jumped, banging my shoulder on the couch. I searched the room for an answer. Father lifted his book.

" 'And God, our Father, has prepared a place for us

filled with wonder upon wonder!'" My voice twanged like a string off-key.

We fell into our ritual, our routine, each of us taking a turn, each of us reading a verse. I let myself sink into the words, into the soothing spell they created. I closed my eyes and let my thoughts float on the vision of heaven that Father's words created.

"What can we learn from this?" Father's voice boomed.

Mortimer answered, but when he spoke, he used a language Father had created when we were children. It was like pig latin, except with a *-hix* instead of an *-ay*. None of us really used it anymore, but Mortimer took the opportunity to make a choice comment about Caspar's little friend.

"Speak in English!" Father whacked the desk. "We have a guest."

"God punishes the wicked," Mortimer amended his comment, shooting Caspar a pleased look.

Father's lip quirked up. "Would you like to read a verse, Amity?"

Mortimer snorted, but Amity ignored him, lifting her book and reading like she had never been intimidated a day in her life.

" 'And once they have taken all they can bear, the end will come swiftly.' "

Caspar looked up, and I swear the gaslight flickered. And I wasn't the only one who noticed it. Everyone seemed to move at once. Caspar fumbled with his book and forced his eyes away.

"Continue, please, Amity." Father's voice wavered slightly. "You have a lovely reading voice."

She continued to read, and Caspar dared to watch her. He watched her read until we heard the rumble of a car engine, rolling down the drive.

" 'And in that day they shall be struck down one by one, and consumed by flames. And when—' "

There was a knock on the door. Father's hand went up. "I think your father has arrived, Amity."

Amity stood slowly. She looked at Caspar, but he kept his head down. She handed Father the book. "Thank you, sir."

The flame sizzled. She left the room. The front door opened and shut. Father gazed at the book she'd given him, turning it in his hand like he thought it might be a fake. Then he set it down and charged toward the door.

Caspar started to rise, but Morty forced him down. "Use your brain!"

The front door flew open, slamming back on its hinges.

His footsteps pounded down the porch steps. *He wouldn't touch her. She doesn't belong to him. He couldn't touch her.*

I looked toward the window, but all I saw were stars. I was afraid to go any closer, afraid of what I would see.

"What exactly do you think you are doing?" My father roared through the void. "Sending her out to spy on me?"

"Gabriel." Michael's voice was calm, light even. "Please. Why would I do that?"

"Because you're trying to destroy me!"

"Why would I want to destroy you, Gabriel?"

Father hissed. "Because you serve the devil."

"Now. That's not very nice."

"And you know it not! That is the tragedy, my dear Michael. The devil works in sinister, insidious ways, and his slaves know not who they are."

"Don't talk like that, please."

"You come to my house—*my house*—and tell me how to speak?" There was a hollow sound as he hit the car.

"Don't act like this in front of my daughter."

"Your *daughter*?" Father said as the engine revved. "She's not your daughter. You don't have children!"

"And you shouldn't have children." I could hear the sound of the tires spitting up the dirt, the engine roaring, then deadening as he drove away.

It wasn't exactly nice, the way Michael Endecott talked about us, like we were a curse. Or worse, a mistake.

When Father came back in, he had broken a sweat. He licked his teeth, then pushed his hair back with the palm of his hand.

"Caspar James Cresswell," he said, and then he said nothing else.

Caspar's eyes were wide and bright, like blue holes burned into his ashen face. For once he didn't have anything to say, no trite words of wisdom, no loosely adapted gospel. What *was* he thinking?

"What were you thinking, bringing that viper into our home?"

"She's not a viper." Wrong point to stick to.

Father moved swiftly across the room. He kicked Caspar so hard that Caspar bounced against Momma's wheelchair. Caspar clung to the arm of the chair for a moment, breath rattling through him; then his arms went slack and he tumbled to the floor.

Before I could see what Caspar would do, if he would forgive Father straightaway or get up and fight, Father kicked him again. Caspar made a wretched sound, choking on a scream. And Father kicked him again. And when Caspar opened his mouth to speak, he spoke in blood.

"Stop it! You're going to kill him!" I heard my own voice scream, but it sounded so stupid, so dramatic. *He wasn't going to kill him. God wouldn't let him.*

I tried to move, but hands held me. Mortimer's hands. I twisted away.

Father kicked Caspar again. Frothy blood spattered across his leather shoes. *This can't be real. This can't be what God wants.*

Father cocked his leg, observing the blood with disdain. I think he expected us not to bleed. He expected us not to be human, his own beautiful, perfect creations.

He shook his foot.

I looked at Hannan, who was the only one of us who, physically, could have stopped Father, but he wasn't even watching. He was reading Father's book, poring over the words at a breakneck pace, like something in those long-dried words might rescue us directly.

We all went to bed early that night. For once, I don't think anyone left their bed. After he finished with Caspar, Father went outside. I went to Caspar immediately, but I was the only one. Momma wheeled herself away from his gasping body, and when Hannan noticed her struggling, he got up and rolled her into her bedroom.

135

"Are you okay?" I brushed Caspar's hair out of his face. It was filmy with dirt from the cave.

He gasped between his bloody teeth, and then, staring at the ceiling like he detected mystic patterns there, he smiled.

"You're such an idiot," Mortimer said. He went upstairs to bed without so much as a backward glance.

I tried to help Caspar sit up, but he went limp in my hands. "I don't know what I was thinking, Castley," he said hoarsely, coughing up a fine spray. I wiped his mouth with the fabric of my dress skirt. Jerusalem and Delvive watched nervously. "Father's right. Father's right to punish me," he assured us, eyes bright. He clung to my arm and lifted himself up so he was leaning against the wall, and me.

"Unbutton your shirt. I need to see your chest." I moved closer to him, wiping the blood from his lips. I thought, strangely, that this was what Father wanted. For all of us to be together. To get everything from one another. *No outsiders.*

He fumbled with the buttons and I bent forward to help him. I reached his navel and pulled the fabric apart. His chest was broad, but his stomach was concave, fringed with rows of ribs. I reminded myself that he hadn't eaten

136

in days, so it wasn't really a hole punched into his stomach, a mark that would last forever.

His skin blanched with the early signs of bruising. I traced my fingers along his bones, trying to pretend I knew what I was doing. "Do you think any of your ribs are broken?" A sob rose in my throat.

"Castley. You had better go. You had better go upstairs." He looked at the three of us girls, watching him with our hearts in our eyes. "Just leave me. It's my own fault. I deserved it."

"But you didn't do anything wrong." A tear broke loose, rolling down my cheek. "You were just trying to help her."

"No," Caspar said, wiping blood from his lips. "I wanted to bring her here. I thought that maybe . . ." I don't know what he thought. That Father would welcome her with open arms? Father wouldn't have welcomed anyone—but Michael Endecott's stepdaughter? He might as well have brought back a Capulet. "And I like her. I do like her." His voice dropped. "In a wicked way." My stomach lurched.

Delvive huffed and got to her feet. She crossed her arms and stood over him. "You shouldn't have done that, Caspar. I never thought I'd say this to you, but how could you be so selfish? You're making trouble for all of us. Don't you think all of us want to do that? Don't you think all of us just wish we could bring some girl home?" *Girl.* I cocked my head, distracted for a moment. "I mean *boy*. Boy or girl." Del blushed. "Just leave him be, Castley! You deserve better." She spun on her heel. I would have laughed if things weren't so dire. I deserved better than my own brother. I heartily agreed.

Baby J stood, then extended her hand toward Caspar, nodding toward the stairs.

"No, I better stay down here," Caspar said. "I better speak to Father when he comes back. I need to ask for his forgiveness."

Anger stung my heart, hard and sharp. What was he doing that for? "Caspar, he could have . . ." But I caught Jerusalem's innocent eyes, and my words turned to dust. Not there, not then. *Not ever,* my brain spat viciously as I got to my feet.

Father didn't forgive Caspar. He didn't punish him. He didn't even speak to him. I was beginning to suspect that Father had more than just Caspar on his mind. The food we'd saved for the End of Days had so depleted that you could see the back wall of the storage shed. The electricity and heating had been cut off a long time ago, but when I went to pour myself a glass of water on Thursday morning, the tap glugged hollowly. We didn't know if the taps were broken or if the water had been cut off, or if, as Father said, God was punishing us for Caspar's lustful thoughts. Because that was what he said, that Caspar's wet dream caused a drought. I wondered if Father had turned the water off himself, but then I felt bad, and then I felt confused.

How was I supposed to tell? How was I supposed to tell what was real and what wasn't? What was God and what was man? Everything was so messed up. The only place I felt half normal was in drama class with George Gray. On Friday we cozied up in our usual place, under the drinking fountain. I had to force myself not to swim in it.

"Hey, can I ask you a question?" I said, stretching my legs and rocking my boots from side to side. "If you don't pay your water bill, does it get cut off?" He was sitting on the floor beside me, playing with his phone.

"I don't know. I don't think so. I think it's illegal. Let's Google it."

"What, you mean, like, on a computer?"

"On my phone." He held up his iPhone. "My phone is like a computer."

"I know that," I said quickly. "I'm not a complete idiot."

"But you don't have a cell phone, do you?" He eyed me wistfully, clutching his phone to his chest.

"No."

"You've never had one?"

"Nope. But we do have a house phone."

"Yeah, I know that." He scratched his nose. "I heard from Amity."

I knocked my boots together. "What do you mean? What does Amity have to do with it?"

"She said she went into your house."

"Well, bully for her."

"Bully?" He nudged my ankle with his foot.

I sat up. "Who is Amity, anyway? I mean, how is she Michael Endecott's stepdaughter when he doesn't even have a wife? How come I've never seen her before?"

"I guess she's the daughter of some girl Mr. Endecott used to date."

"Where's her mom?"

"Jail. Apparently." He shrugged. "That's why she moved here. I guess Mr. Endecott is, like, really nice or something; he just basically adopted her."

Beyond the glass, Tommy and Bobby were smoking again. Tommy was chewing tobacco at the same time, spitting it into an empty Mountain Dew bottle.

"Well, maybe he should just mind his own business." I couldn't help thinking about what he'd said to my father, that he shouldn't have had children. Michael Endecott thought I shouldn't even exist. "Hey, let's go out and have a cigarette."

"You don't smoke!" He took my arm.

"Yes, I do. I mean, I have before. I know what I'm doing." I wrestled my arm away and walked to the door. "Are you coming or what?"

If Tommy and Bobby were surprised to see me approach, they were shocked when I opened my mouth and asked for a cigarette. Tommy actually sat up straight, which, trust me, never happened.

"Of course," Bobby said, pulling out a Parliament.

"I love Parliaments," I said. I don't know why. "Are you gonna have one?" I asked George.

"Not likely."

Tommy held out a light. His hand shook slightly, but it may have been the tobacco overdose. He lit my cigarette. And then the three of them watched me smoke.

I finished half the cigarette before anyone spoke. "You look so cool doing that." It was Tommy. He looked impressed. "It's, like, Amish gone wrong." People were always comparing my family to Amish people, which made me think they didn't really know what Amish was.

George Gray kept his voice down. "Aren't you not supposed to smoke?" Jeez. Even he was afraid of Father.

"No one is supposed to smoke," I said. "That's kind of the point."

Tommy laughed—a hard bark.

George took my arm possessively. "Do you wanna go back inside?"

"I'm still smoking." I held up my rapidly depleting cigarette.

"Hey, is it true you guys believe that you're the only people who get to go to heaven?" Bobby asked.

That was probably one of the most sacred things Father ever talked about: the afterlife and how wonderful it would be for us, and how bad it would be for everyone else. "Yep," I said. Why not?

"Sucks to be us, I guess," Bobby said. I knew he was only saying it because he was coming on to me. We held a weird fascination for the seedier boys, we Cresswell girls. I was savvy enough to know it was a sex thing. It wasn't like they really cared about us, like they would actually want to be in a relationship with a freak.

"Yeah. I don't know," I said. My cigarette was out, but I hid it so George wouldn't notice. "So. Do you guys know about any parties this weekend?"

George's eyes practically popped out of his head. "You can't go to a party!"

"Why not?"

"Because you said you were gonna hang out with me." He took my cigarette and stubbed it out for me. "Castley, come on. We need to go pick our scene now."

"I don't like to be told what to do."

He put his hands up. "All right, fine. Do whatever you want."

I looked at Tommy and Bobby, who both decided to leer at me at the same time. I looked at George. "Okay. I'll go with you."

We went to the bookshelves, where Mrs. Fein kept all the plays and scene books. "Do you want to do funny or dramatic?" George said, dropping smoothly into Indian style.

I sat on a lone desk and rested my chin on my hands. "Hey. Why don't you like those guys? I thought they were popular."

"They are popular. They're also casual rapists."

I fingered my hair. "How can you rape someone casually?"

"I didn't say they raped anyone casually," he said, and for once, his face was serious. "I mean they're casual about rape."

"Do you know someone or—"

"I don't know anyone personally. But, yeah, I know for definite. You should stay away from guys like that."

"We were just talking."

"But you shouldn't even . . . Castley, I know this might sound like an asshole statement, but there are people that do really bad shit, okay? And you shouldn't just be friends with them, or hang out with them sometimes. You shouldn't tolerate them at all. You should just cut them out of your life completely. Life's too short, and there are tons of nice people you could be spending your time with." It was pretty clear he meant him specifically.

I cleared my throat. "I think you're wrong."

"Castley, I know for a fact—"

"No, I mean about there being nice people. There aren't any nice people. Father . . ." I took a deep breath. "Father always says that the world is a really cold place, and he's totally right." George frowned, but kept quiet. "I remember when . . . when they put us all in homes—you probably heard about it anyway. I learned something then that I think is true, always. People don't actually care about other people. They just don't. Even if you just listen to people when they're talking, when they're trying to have a conversation." I motioned to our classmates as

144

they chattered away in pairs, laughing or frowning or making fake gagging sounds. "One person tells a story about themselves and then the other person does the same thing, and neither of them realizes they're not even talking to each other. They're just talking to themselves out loud. Like sometimes at night, I would cry and this woman would come in and tell me about the times she was scared, or the times she was sad, or how hard her life was. She didn't understand what I'd been through. She didn't understand what I was going through. She didn't even want to know. No one does. Except your family. Your family are the only people who listen. Your family are the only people who understand. Your family are the only people who really care."

"Wow." George Gray sat back. "That is the most I have ever heard you say." He shook his head. "And I can't even argue with you, because what you said has absolutely nothing to do with what I was talking about."

nine

I meant what I said to George about family, but right then my family didn't feel like the safest place. All of us children were in the yard that afternoon trying to organize pieces to take to the market that Saturday. But instead of working together, we were falling apart.

Delvive had been trying to spruce up a dresser for over an hour, but she kept falling into spaced-out reveries. Hannan was spending more time scowling and grunting at her than doing any actual work.

He snorted in disgust. "Del. No one is going to buy that thing. It's moldy. Once you get mold, it never goes away. It's just going to eat the whole thing up."

"You should know, Mr. Athlete's Foot," she spat back.

Hannan mumbled something that sounded suspiciously like "I can't help it if I live in a shithole."

"Besides, I'm getting rid of the mold." Del lifted a spatula over her head. "Once you get rid of the mold, you don't have mold anymore."

Hannan put down the tin kettle he was supposed to be repairing. "You shouldn't be focusing on big furniture, either. It takes up too much space in the truck, and people don't buy it. You should be trying to find small things. Small things that people can afford."

"There aren't any small things." Del motioned across the expanse of busted furniture, broken tents, and moth-eaten office chairs.

"What about your record player?" Hannan said. Delvive had a record player upstairs. She only had two records—Brahms and medieval lute—but she worshiped it like it was God.

"It's *my* record player."

"You should sell that."

Delvive staggered to her feet. "Seriously? Seriously? You think there's, like, some huge market for record players? You really think my getting rid of it would be worth the two bucks someone would pay for it?" She was close to tears. She gaped around, looking for help. Caspar was far out in the yard, working with a deranged intensity. Mortimer was helping Jerusalem bang a metal tub back into place.

"She's right, Hannan," I volunteered. "I doubt anyone would want it, anyway. It's lopsided. Plus normal people have iPhones."

Hannan met my eyes and then tossed the kettle across the yard. It landed in a plastic kiddie pool filled with mold. The others looked up. "This is all a joke! This is all a waste of time!"

"Just take a break, Hannan," Caspar called out with his stupid over-cheeriness.

Hannan batted his hand through the air as though he were pushing us all away. "Father should make it so you get to keep whatever money you make. Then people might actually do the work." And with that he strolled back into the house.

I continued working. I was painting a chair "distressed" green in the hopes that no one would notice the wood was starting to splinter.

Delvive sniveled. "Do you really think I should sell my record player? Father never lets me keep good records, anyway. If it would help, I . . ." She sat down on the ground and cried.

I watched the paint dry on the end of my brush, then dropped it in the water I'd taken from the pool. I walked over and sat down next to Del. "If you want to keep it, keep it. You're right. I don't think it would make any difference."

I gazed across the yard, at Caspar working like a slave, at Mortimer banging on the metal tub like a demon possessed.

Delvive wiped her eyes with the back of her hand. "Why are things so bad? It doesn't seem fair. I look at the people at school and think, didn't we have it bad enough already? And it just keeps getting worse."

"This, too, shall pass," I said. "Right? They'll go to the market this weekend and make a ton of money and everything will be better again."

"But who'll go with Father? I don't think he's gonna want Caspar after . . . after what happened last night. And I don't . . ." She paused to sob. "I don't want to go, because if anything goes wrong, it'll be my fault."

"It'll be fine," I said, fixing her hair. "Father will forgive Caspar, and they'll bring Jerusalem, and she'll do one of her paintings. It's always worked out before, so we don't have any reason to believe it won't work now. We just have to have faith. That's all."

Delvive looked at me with a tear-streaked face. "I don't think Father will ever forgive Caspar."

"I'll talk to him," I said. I think she thought I meant Father, but I didn't. Even I wasn't that brave.

Caspar worked through dinner. There wasn't enough to go around, so he volunteered to fast. I needed to talk to him, so I did the same. He was making something out of broken wood pieces, dresser legs and chair struts, and it was only then, in the dark, that I realized it was a birdcage, big enough for a person to crawl inside.

"Gosh, that's really beautiful," I said as he lifted it up and it spun in his hand.

His smile looked like a bruise in the dark. "I'm glad you're out here. I need to ask you something. But first I need to apologize."

I sat down on an old office chair, feeling unsteady on my feet. "You don't have to apologize," I said. "You didn't do anything wrong."

"Yes, I did." He took a deep breath. "We've always been taught that everything is fate, and sometimes I think it's easy to forget that the devil works in fate, too." My stomach dropped.

"What do you mean? I don't understand." I hated,

absolutely hated, when people mentioned the devil, espe- cially after dark. It was like I could feel his malign spirit, pushed up against the edges of my consciousness. *God and the devil are playing inside you.*

"Amity," he said, his voice long on the vowels. "I was in God's Chambers and she just appeared, right at sunset, like it was preordained. And I'd been . . . I may as well tell you that I put myself down there because I was hav- ing lustful thoughts about her. I didn't mean to, but it just happened. Just like that, when I wasn't paying attention."

The chair squeaked.

I felt a twinge of jealousy. Not because Amity was pretty or even because she was prettier than me (which she was), but because she had that confidence, that con- fidence that I would never have.

"So when she showed up, I guess I thought—no, I *hoped* that there was a reason for it. I hoped that it was fate, and I thought if I took her home maybe, maybe, maybe it was supposed to happen. But I lied to myself. I told myself it was fate when really it was just what I *wanted* fate to be, you see? I tried to force fate."

For the first time, maybe ever in his life, Caspar looked desperate and confused. He looked like the rest of us: helpless, maybe even a little pathetic. Weak. But instead of reproach, I felt a vibrant sense of longing, and I couldn't tell if I was longing for him or longing for him to get what he wanted, instead of what God wanted, for once.

I rocked myself left and right in the office chair, so it creaked and squeaked like the spell of a wicked witch.

Caspar's expression dropped. "Mortimer says she's an agent of the devil, leading me into temptation."

"Well, Mortimer would know."

Caspar put the birdcage down. "It's not that I don't believe anymore or that I'm questioning it or anything like that. I'm just . . ." He took a strange breath. "I'm just *attracted* to her. And that's wrong."

I breathed deeply, but it hurt going down. "I think it's normal." I gazed out at the treetops and the stars placed above, like the stars on the trees, put there to decorate the universe. To make it feel like a safe and beautiful place. "Caspar, do you ever think about what Father says, about how we're destined to be together in heaven?"

"Yes."

I couldn't speak for a while. I tried to count to ten, but the numbers were jumbled. "But don't you think that's wrong? I mean, we're brother and sister."

"It would be wrong on earth. But heavenly laws are different from earthly ones."

"Okay, but what about, you know, *sex*?"

Caspar frowned as though it were a grave consideration. "I don't know if there is sex in heaven."

"I'm not talking about heaven," I said, concentrating on the stars as they seemed to smear and come apart before my eyes. "I'm talking about now. I mean, none of us will ever have sex. I don't mean with each other. I mean with anyone. What if we live to be a hundred? What about the future? Do you ever think about that? Are we all just going to live forever in this house together? What about... I mean, Father will die one day. It happens. That's what happens."

He was quiet for a long time. I think he was shocked by what I'd said, or else he was trying to disassemble it so he could push the reality away like we all did, all the time. Eventually he said, "I don't think we need to worry about that. I don't think life will be for us like it is for other people."

He was right. How could it be the same? It hadn't started the same, and it couldn't end the same. We were Cresswells. We weren't like other people and we never would be. "Not ever?"

"I don't think so." And then he hugged me quickly, but he held on longer. We both gazed at the same stars. "Castley? I need you to do something for me. For us."

153

"Okay."

He pulled away, holding me out in front of him. "I want you to go with Father this weekend."

My heart lurched. I didn't want to go with Father to the market. I didn't want the responsibility. I didn't want to sit there while people stared. "But what if he wants you?"

"He doesn't—he won't want me. Castley, Father is extremely angry with me. I don't think that's going to change any time soon. Will you go in my place?"

I wanted to tell him that I couldn't. That it wasn't possible. That I couldn't smile at strangers, that I couldn't sell myself or anything else. But Caspar had asked me to, so I said yes.

As I took my seat in Drama the next day, I couldn't stop thinking about the market. I had volunteered myself after scriptures last night. I'd hoped Father would say no, but he'd agreed right away. And now I could feel my whole body tightening.

I hunched over my desk, fingers curling around the edge.

"You okay?" George Gray sat down beside me, with the same stupid contented look on his face. "Hey, my friends and I are going into Huxley tomorrow to get stuff for Homecoming. Amity's coming, I think."

"Why would I care if Amity's going?"

"Because isn't she, like, with your brother or something?"

I sat up. "Why do you say that?"

"Because I see them together all the time."

"What do you mean? When?"

"Like, I don't know, this morning. I thought they were, like, dating or something."

"I didn't know that." I couldn't believe Caspar was still hanging out with her after everything that happened, after everything he'd said. After what he'd said just last night, about how wicked it was.

"So, you wanna come with us?"

"No."

He frowned, but even his frown looked happy. "But I thought you said you wanted to hang out?"

"I didn't say that. I didn't say I *wanted* to hang out. And anyway, I can't."

"Why not? Are you not allowed?" I hated how gleeful all the things I wasn't allowed to do seemed to make him. Like it was all some great joke.

"I have to go to the market with Father."

155

"Which market?"

"Fall Fling or something. I don't know; it's some stupid festival where we sell stuff."

"What do you sell?" He scooted forward in his chair.

I could tell he thought it was some cute, crafty thing we Cresswells did. Like we might sell embossed pillows or personalized door signs, not damaged furniture and old appliances Father picked up in front yards and landfills.

Last night Father came back with tanks full of water and very strict rules about when and how we were supposed to use them. That morning Caspar had made an arrangement with Miss Syrup, his cooking teacher, whereby we could come in before school and eat the leftovers. It was humiliating, but we were all so hungry that none of us cared.

"Whatever," I said. "We sell whatever Father finds on the side of the road." I almost told him we were broke. I almost told him about the water and about Miss Syrup.

"That's cool," he said. I don't know how he arrived at that conclusion. I let my mind drift away, away from him and there. I could see Caspar's birdcage spinning in the dark.

"Hey! I found us a scene," he said. I shot him a look.

Thanks for letting me pick, buddy. I guess everyone automatically knew that I didn't have a choice, in anything. "Don't look at me like that; I picked it for you." He reached into his clean, new backpack and pulled out a crumpled playbook. "*A Doll's House.* It reminded me of you."

He put it on my desk, so I flopped it over and read the back cover. It was about a husband who underestimated his wife. "Why does this remind you of me?"

"Because you look like a doll."

I hadn't been to the market since I was a little girl. When we were younger, Father would bring as many of us as possible. We used to draw people in because we dressed in tiny bonnets and pilgrim-type pinafores. It was cute on a child. On a teenager going through puberty, it was just embarrassing.

We all woke up at three the next morning to pack the truck. Jerusalem climbed into the back with the birdcage and some burnt-out kitchenware, and I sat in the front seat next to Father. His eyes were clouded so they looked almost moldy as we drove through the semidarkness toward the market.

Father had taken the radio out of the truck in a pique of violence. He said that any kind of transmission could be manipulated by the spirit of the devil—radios, TVs, cell phones—so you didn't know whether you were listening to actual people or if the devil had slipped in to deejay.

But as we drove past Huxley and into Grousman, I wondered if the devil even needed a radio. There was a bad spirit in the car, like there was in the house. Father claimed he was a conduit for spirits and visions—good and bad. He said it was a blessing, but right then I wished he weren't quite so blessed.

Baby J was no help. She didn't say a word, just sat in the back and watched the window. I didn't know how we were expected to sell anything, with Father occupied by an evil spirit and Baby J speechless and me trying to swallow my growing disenchantment.

As we drove, on and on through the woods, I felt like we were a curse, my whole family, like we were a stain and a curse on the earth.

I tried to think *What would Caspar do?* as I helped Father set up. But it was a lot harder to be like Caspar than he made it look. I tried to smile, but my smile kept slipping. I tried to look pretty, because I thought that might pull people in, but the fetching patterns in my fabric weren't exactly a huge draw in the twenty-first century.

Jerusalem sat down in the grass and painted, but that day her brush was limp and her colors were dark, and from what I could tell, she was painting a black hole.

Father was the worst. He just sat in the front seat of the truck with his hair awry and his lips twisted up. It was almost like he wanted us to fail.

A group of college-aged boys approached. I stepped forward, arms folded tight around my middle. "Good morning," I practically whispered.

They looked at one another and sniggered. One of them stood back, like he was surveying our wares. "Did you raid a dump, or what?"

The others laughed, but I didn't even feel it, and somehow that seemed worse. "We have good prices." I heard my own words echo in my head, and I wanted to kick myself. I sounded desperate. I sounded pathetic.

"I bet you do," one of them said, leering. I glanced back at Father, but all I could see was the back of his head inside the truck. I shivered.

They just stood there stupidly, waiting for me to say something so they could insult me again, and I hated them; for once I hated someone else more than I hated myself.

"You know what?" I said. "Fuck you. You're all a bunch

of fucking assholes." Baby J looked up, eyes wide. "You seriously think I give a fuck what you think? If you don't want to buy anything, fuck off."

The ringleader held his hands up. "Jesus, way to over-react. We were just kidding. Take a chill pill."

"What a freak," another muttered.

"Just fuck off. We don't need your fucking money."

"Freak."

"Bitch."

They unloaded the rest of their insults and then they left. My fingers shook. I pressed them against my ribs. I glanced at the back of Father's head. He was frozen, either asleep or in one of his trances. Baby J kept painting.

I sighed, and I felt it roll through me like giving up. I folded down in the grass beside Jerusalem.

"What are you painting?"

She looked at me. Blinked.

"You know, Mrs. Tulle came up to me the other day to talk about your paintings." I reached down and yanked a dandelion out by the roots. I wasn't usually so unnec-essarily cruel to living things, but I felt angry. I felt an anger I didn't think I could swallow. "She said you hid them. Because you didn't want her to show them to any-body."

Baby J went back to painting, purposefully ignoring me.

"Don't you think people might want to see them?" I tried again. "Don't you think they're worth showing?"

She said nothing. She just kept painting, painting pictures to keep hidden, stacked in a pile at the back of our bedroom.

I forced myself to my feet. What was the point? I wanted to cry, but I knew that if I did, no one would care—not Father or Jerusalem or all the strangers, who thought we were nothing because we said we were.

The day didn't go any better from there. Father never left the truck. Baby J finished her painting and spent the rest of her time staring into space, and all the shoppers gave us a wide berth. I knew it was partly my fault, but it was like I couldn't stop. I hated them, I hated all of them, and I couldn't hide it and they all felt it. They all knew it. I don't know what Caspar was thinking, telling me to volunteer for the job. I felt guilty for letting him down, and that only made things worse.

It was like something was broken inside me, and the worst part was, I was pretty sure it had been broken for a long time. When you're hanging on by a thread, you don't even notice until that thread starts to break.

The only thing we sold was Caspar's birdcage, which was the only thing I wanted to keep. It was funny how fate worked that way sometimes, like a trick. Like everything you wanted, you didn't get, and everything you didn't want, you got in spades.

As we drove home that evening, the evil spirit felt stronger, and I was pretty sure it was in me, too.

Father cleared his throat as we wound through the trees. "In the past, God has always provided for us—down to the letter, exactly what we needed, God has given us. And now, he isn't. What do you think that means?"

I sighed. "That he's testing us?"

Father shook his head. *Try again.*

"That he's punishing us?"

"No." He spoke carefully, as though it were a very simple matter. "If God provides to keep us alive, and he stops providing, what does that mean?"

My shoulders bristled. I looked back at Jerusalem, but she was staring out the window with starved, hollow eyes.

When we got home, Father didn't even bother unloading the car. Caspar met us on the porch. His eyes passed quickly over the truck.

"Caspar," Father said. "I want you to gather everyone in the family room. There is something I have to tell you. I have been keeping it to myself because I hoped I might be wrong. But I can see now that it must be shared, to break this boil that our lives have become. To liberate us, at last."

Caspar's eyes passed over mine as he turned back toward the house. He felt it, too. Something was about to happen. Finally.

ten

In spite of everything, a funny hopefulness accompanied us into the family room that night. Something needed to change, and God recognized that, and Father recognized that, and one of them would provide.

The six of us sat close, tight, at our father's feet. Our mother kept quiet in the corner. All of us wanted to escape. And one of them would provide.

"I had a vision," Father began, brushing the cover of one of the books stacked in a pyramid on the corner table. "Some time ago, but I was afraid to share it. Afraid because what I saw terrified me. I hoped that it was not from God, but I see now that God is punishing us. God is punishing all of us for fearing his vision. For fearing his wisdom."

My eyes caught Caspar's, remembering my dream. Had I had the same vision?

Father's hands contracted, once, and then his shoulders dropped, and he spoke with a sigh that seemed to come from the end of the world. "We have tarried on this earth long enough," he said meekly. "And soon God will be calling us home."

All eyes widened, but not one breath caught. Not one flicker of dissent was heard. My heart skipped in my chest and then began to beat, like a clock counting down.

What does that mean? Soon God will be calling us home.

I couldn't sleep that night; I could barely think straight. As soon as I could control myself enough to walk, I walked out of the bedroom, down the stairs, and into the woods. I wasn't alone. Caspar and Hannan and Mortimer were already there. I found them in a clearing we'd decorated as children, with a fire pit and rocks gathered in a circle.

"Where're Del and Baby J?" Caspar said. His hands were clasped in front of him like he was holding an invisible gun.

"I think they're asleep. I don't know. I think they're afraid."

"We're here." Del appeared behind me. She led Baby J into the circle.

Mortimer was smoking wildly, but no one commented. No one spoke at all.

"Do you think . . ." My voice faded. I licked my lips to taste the traces.

"What about your dream?" Caspar said. I wanted to kick him. "About the fire?"

My eyes bored into him. "It was just a dream, Caspar."

"Maybe it wasn't," Del said suddenly, crazily. "You should tell us. It might help us figure out what's going on."

"It was just a dream."

"Just tell it," Hannan ordered. They were all glaring at me, all five of them, like this was somehow my fault.

"Fine, but it was . . ." I stopped, took a breath. "I dreamed we were at Homecoming. We were at the Homecoming game and we were all standing on Father's truck, and there was a fire and . . . that's it."

"Homecoming," Hannan repeated, as though it were a clue.

"But it was just a dream. I think it . . ." I was almost going to say that it had more to do with my growing fear of Father than it did with any kind of bad omen, but I looked around the circle and I knew that I couldn't. They believed it. All of them still believed it. And maybe I did, too.

"Caspar, what do you think?" Hannan said. Caspar was the one we all deferred to, but for once I was scared of what he might say. I thought about what George Gray had said, about how he was still hanging out with Amity. Maybe Caspar wasn't perfect. Maybe he didn't have all the answers.

"If God really does have a plan for us, then all we can do is attend his mercy."

"But how do you know it's God?" I burst out. Again, their eyes were on me. Again, I felt they didn't trust me. Again, I wondered if I could trust myself.

"We ask him," Caspar said. "We should all pray."

A murmur of assent passed through the group, and they all moved forward at once to get down on their knees in the dirt. I followed them, without thinking, and took Caspar's hand.

"Dear God, we ask for you to give us strength, whatever your plans for us," he began, which wasn't really the same as asking God if he wanted us to die.

There was a terrible serenity in our house all day Sunday. Everyone was kinder to one another, as though we expected to vanish at any moment. Mortimer told Father about my dream, which seemed to please him to no end. Caspar barely left my side. I guess he thought we better start courting if we were going to be married in heaven.

All I wanted was to be alone. I couldn't stop thinking about George Gray and Amity and Lisa Perez, going shopping for Homecoming in Huxley. How lucky they were to not be lucky or blessed or exceptional. To just be like everybody else.

We went out to the lake in the afternoon, all six of us Cresswell children, and we swam and we played and we soaked ourselves with life. Then Caspar and I collapsed on the beach and gazed at the sky as though we could see the stars through the sunlight.

"It's funny, isn't it?" he said, chest contracting as he caught his breath. "How beautiful the world becomes when you think you might have to leave it?"

I don't want to leave it. It felt like a burr inside my chest. "Yeah," I said. "It's really not so bad after all."

He took my hand, and I felt the same thrill I felt when anyone touched me, because I wasn't touched enough. "I'm glad I have you, Castley."

"I'm glad I have you, too." He clung tighter to my hand,

so tight I wondered if he might be free-falling, somewhere in his mind.

I watched my brothers and sisters swimming in the lake with the sky superimposed over them, hazy on the water.

Monday was unseasonably warm, so George Gray and I went outside to run lines. I was in a strange mood. I mean, I was in a good mood and I thought that was strange. Life had taken on a peculiar unreal quality, and it was making me act in a way I never had before. I climbed onto a brick wall at the end of the courtyard so I could have a stellar view of the sewer below.

George climbed up after me. "Are you auditioning for *Macbeth*?"

"I don't know. Mrs. Fein basically offered my sisters and me the roles of the three witches, but Jerusalem doesn't speak, so . . ."

"Yeah. Well. You should do it. You're a really good actress."

"You've hardly even seen me act."

He cocked his head, his eyes oddly wise. "You're acting all the time."

My balance wavered and I caught him by the shoulder.

He reached over and took my hand, to steady me maybe, but he kept on holding it, even though he was holding my left hand with his left hand and it felt awkward.

"Do you like being alive?" I scooted closer to him without meaning to.

"That's a weird question."

"I just mean, like, overall. What do you think about it?"

He cocked a smile. "Overall? Yeah, I like it. I mean, it's all we've got, right?"

"Well, what about heaven?"

"Nobody knows if heaven even exists." He shrugged, tapping his heels along the stone.

"What if you knew for sure it did? And you knew for sure it was better than here?"

"I don't know. I guess I'd still want to stay here as long as I could."

"But why?"

"Just 'cuz. I'm here now. And I like it." He squeezed my hand. "You know, I really think you would like hanging out with me and my friends. I really think you would. I think that you . . . I mean, I know you guys have all your weird rules and stuff, but you should really see more of the world than you do, in my opinion. I mean, don't you want to choose your own life?"

I sniffed. "You can't choose your own life. You're born into it. Your life chooses you."

"Not when you grow up. You're almost seventeen, right? I mean, you're practically an adult. Once you turn eighteen, you can do whatever you want."

I almost said that I might never turn eighteen, but I didn't.

Isn't it convenient that Father's dream happened now, before we have the chance to get away? I shoved the thought down. It was horrible, too horrible. It was a wicked, evil thought. *You had the same vision.*

Riva and Lisa were in my CPM group, which was about as awful as it sounded. But that day their teasing didn't bother me. In fact, when Riva said, "How the hell do you get your hair to look like that?" I just smiled distantly. *We have tarried on this earth long enough. See ya later, Riva.*

"I love the way you guys do your hair," Lisa said, scooting closer to me. "Hey, Castley? You know we're having a bonfire tonight, and you should absolutely, definitely come. Bring your brother."

As sad as it is to say, it was practically the first time anyone outside my family had invited me anywhere. And even though I knew she was using me to get to Mortimer, I could feel myself opening up, and I knew I really wanted to go.

"Which brother?" Riva asked. "Caspar's the only hot one, but he's such a nerd, oh my God."

"Mortimer." Lisa sighed.

"Eww, Mortimer, are you for real?" Riva spun around to face me. "Is Mortimer actually an albino? Because I actually have no idea what an albino looks like."

"I have no fucking idea."

Riva smiled in spite of herself. "Did you just swear? Oh my God, that was so funny. I'm totally gonna put in my status that I heard a Cresswell say the *F* word. People will die."

Lisa ducked down closer to me. "Anyway, you guys should come. It's tonight. You should just come. Seize the day, or something."

Even though I had always told myself that I hated Riva and the rest of them, I couldn't refuse them at close range. I tried to tell myself that it was part of God's plan. *Sometimes you have to remind yourself that what you think you're missing out on really isn't so great.*

And what did it matter? It would all be over soon anyway, I thought with a shiver. I wanted to go. I wanted to see what life was like for normal people, for real people. I wanted to go. Just 'cuz.

"Yeah. Sure," I said, before she could change her mind. "Just tell me where it is."

When I found out where it was, I knew I needed to change my mind sharpish. But I felt reckless and hopeless and wanting. I caught up with Mortimer on the way home. He didn't look happy about it.

Mortimer had been acting strangely ever since the fire. I knew he was mad at Caspar for hanging out with Michael Endecott's stepdaughter. Mortimer hated Michael, maybe more than any of us did, for taking him to the hospital, for forcing the family apart. I had never really thought about how it must have been for Mortimer, trapped in the hospital, alone, in pain. The way they must have asked him *What happened? What happened?* When he knew that all of our futures, our *family*, was wrapped up in the answer.

"Hey," I said carefully, keeping pace when he sped up. "We haven't really hung out in a while. How do you feel about a bonfire?" Shit. I couldn't believe I'd just asked him to go to a *fire*.

His lip curled. "What bonfire?"

173

"I don't know." I tried to keep my voice light. "Is there more than one bonfire?"

"No, I mean, who asked you?" He looked at me like he knew the answer.

I took a deep breath. "Lisa. Lisa asked me if we wanted to go to a bonfire."

"She asked you or she asked 'we'?"

"She asked me. . . . And she asked me to ask you."

"*Quelle surprise.* Why don't you tell Lisa that I would rather pierce my own scrotum?"

"I don't think I will."

He smiled briefly, a flash in the pan, and then his expression soured. "You know she's using you, right?"

"Yes." I gritted my teeth.

"You know she doesn't care about us. You know none of them do. She's a bone collector. A superfan. You know she has a book about us? Like, a little diary where she writes down all the rules, all the things people say, like we're something that should be kept under glass." He leaned back to gauge my reaction. "That's how Amity knew where to find Caspar. Lisa told her where to go, if you wanna fuck a Cresswell."

I let him finish. "Why are you talking like this? What happened?"

His eyes shone with a milky light. "Nothing happened. That's the problem. Something is supposed to happen, but nothing ever does."

I left my bed at nine o'clock. I ran through the woods like I was chasing my own soul. I wanted everything now. I wanted life to happen *now*, and quickly, before I missed it. I would have done anything to stop myself from thinking about the ticking of the clock.

I went to Lisa's house first because the bonfire wasn't happening until later. She lived in a trailer on Emily Higgins's estate. I knew where it was because Caspar and I had once cleared a snow path there.

"You're here," Lisa said, opening the door. "Is Mortimer with you?"

I shook my head. "He might come later," I lied.

"Okay, cool." She smiled, stepping aside to let me in. "I'm glad you're here." I tried not to think about the book, to look for it. So what if she had a book? I used to keep a diary. It was probably something she did for fun. It didn't mean what Mortimer thought it meant. It didn't mean we were freaks.

Lisa led me through the trailer. She had her own room at the back, with a bubbly pink television. Emily was getting ready to the sound of music videos.

She jumped back when she saw me. "Oh my gosh, Del! What are you doing here?" She sounded angry.

"I'm not Delvive; I'm Castley."

"Oh." She pressed her hand into her chest as though pushing her heart back into place. "Oh, gosh. Jeez, you gave me a fright."

"Sorry. You and Del are scene partners, right?"

She made a face. "Um, yeah."

"Do you not like her?"

"Castley, I'm a Christian."

"No. Sorry. I just meant . . . You just seemed really surprised when you saw me. I thought maybe you didn't get along, that's all." I felt my cheeks color.

"We get along fine," she snapped.

My experiment wasn't going well. Wherever I went, I couldn't seem to escape my family. I tried to focus on the TV screen.

"Do you want me to turn that off?" Lisa asked.

Some practically naked girl was gyrating to a pop song, but I shook my head. "No." I debated whether I should tell them my plan, my devious plan to live the whole night like I was just a normal girl. "No, it's cool. Can I ask you a favor, though? Can I borrow your clothes— just for tonight?" I tried to swallow the weird kick of guilt. *Just do it. Just pretend to be someone else. Please.*

"Oh my gosh, yes, totally! That would be awesome! We can do a makeover. We can take pictures, like Before and After, right, Emily?"

"I guess." Emily seemed deflated. I wondered if she would have preferred Delvive.

"I don't want pictures."

"Oh my gosh." Lisa grabbed her heart. "Do you believe they'll take your soul?"

"I don't want to talk about what I believe."

Lisa frowned, like she was debating what to do with me. "Okay . . . Let's talk about clothes. What do you want to wear?"

I breathed a sigh of relief. "Um, okay . . ." I wanted it to be perfect. I wanted whatever I wore to be perfect. The dream outfit, the dream life. I wanted it all, just for one night. "Do you have jean shorts?" I had been obsessed with jean shorts ever since I was little. Cutoff jean shorts and a T-shirt that actually fit. I would keep my boots.

"Yeah, of course, I have, like, ten pairs." She went to her dresser and tossed pairs onto the bed next to Emily. "Pick whichever ones you want."

I picked the shortest, most faded pair. I wanted to go change in private, but I'd passed the bathroom on the way in and I knew it was too small. Instead I removed my long underwear in the corner, trying to stuff it into a ball before anyone saw. Which was pretty much impossible when they were both staring at me.

"Do you want to borrow underwear or something?" Lisa said. "I seriously don't care. I wash my clothes and everything."

I mouthed the word *yes* and she brought me panties and a bra.

"You can keep them," she said, standing so close I could smell her candy breath.

"Thanks," I said hoarsely.

She just smiled. "Can I unbraid your hair? I bet you have the prettiest hair." I nodded. She waited for me to change into the underwear and shorts, which was easy to do under my enormous dress.

I still had the photograph of teenage Father in my pocket. I was afraid my brothers and sisters would find it and make me destroy it, so I transferred it from dress to dress every morning. I made sure to hide it in the back pocket of Lisa's shorts.

I took the dress off so I was standing there in cutoffs and a bra. I tried not to stare at my reflection in the window. I had never seen myself so bare. We didn't have mirrors at our house. Father said they led to vanity, and

I could feel a certain enchantment as I reached up, inside the mirror, and touched the tips of my tied-off hair.

"Come sit next to me," Lisa directed. I put a shirt on and sat in front of her on the bed, the same way I did with Del and Baby J every morning, and I let her unbraid my hair.

Emily offered to do my makeup. "I promise to make it natural. You already have such pretty features."

And all I could think the whole time was, *This is what it's like to be a normal girl, this is what it's like to be a normal girl.* I thought it so hard and so fast that I never got the chance to just enjoy it.

eleven

When they finished, I wasn't just trying to be a normal girl in my mind; I was one on the outside, too. I won't say I looked pretty because I wasn't a pretty girl, but I did look sort of striking. Most of that was down to my hair, which went past my waist and was thick and curly and almost silvery in color. I was so frail without all the fabric to hide behind that my hair looked more alive than I did.

"You look amazing," Lisa said. "You know, you could probably sell your hair for, like, three hundred bucks."

I immediately thought of my family, desperate for money, and then my stomach crinkled like tinfoil. "Hey, can you guys do me a favor? Can you not mention to anyone that I'm a Cresswell?"

They looked at each other. "Um . . . no offense, but they go to our school. They're gonna know you're a Cresswell."

I didn't really agree with her. In my experience, people didn't look closely at one another. Especially at us Cresswell kids, who seemed to fade into the background of everyone else's lives. George Gray was the only boy at school (that I wasn't related to) who actually knew my first name.

"That's fine. That's fine if they do, but don't tell them."

Lisa shrugged and smiled, like it might be fun. "What should we call you?"

"You can still call me Castley."

"Why?" Emily Higgins said, resting her chin on her hand. "Why don't you want anyone to know you're a Cresswell?"

"I just want to be someone else."

"Are you kidding?" Lisa crossed her hand over her heart. "I would die to be a Cresswell."

We drove down to the bonfire in Emily Higgins's truck. I knew the way through the woods, knew the way by heart, but driving was different.

"Do either of you smoke?" I asked. I thought I'd better

get into character now, and my character smoked. My character didn't know the difference between good rules and bad rules, so she broke them all with equal splendor.

"No, but someone down there will have cigarettes," Emily offered.

"And weed." Lisa turned backward in the front seat. "You really should put on a coat, you know? There's gonna be a fire, but it's freakin' cold outside."

"No, I don't want to wear a jacket," I maintained. That wasn't the point. In order for this to work, I needed to see myself, outside myself, exactly as I wanted to be. I wanted to create an image of a night that would stay with me forever, and a jacket would ruin it.

We pulled up in the parking lot, squeezing into a row of trucks. It looked like any old parking lot. *And Father says this is a sacred place.* Above the tree line, the black spires of the castle poked a hole in the night sky.

I followed them out of the car and up the dirt path that led to the amphitheater. We came around the back, and I couldn't stop my eyes from passing over the sewer grate. *What if one of them is down there? What if Caspar volunteered himself in the middle of the night?* I told myself that he wasn't, that he hadn't, but then I thought about what Father taught us, that the cave was a passageway to heaven, that God was close there, that if you prayed hard enough, the rocks would glow.

I stopped to slow my heartbeat.

"You okay, Cass?" I felt Lisa's fingers brush my bare arm. There was something about human touch that always pulled me out of my head. I guess because I craved it so much.

She grinned at me, and I thought about her and Mortimer kissing, there, outside the cave. I wondered if a place could be more than one place at any one time. If there could be separate dimensions, or threads, laid one on top of another, so the world was a trillion different worlds all at once, a different world for each individual person, all of them overlapping, sometimes clashing. I thought all this, and I hadn't even smoked weed.

"Let's go," I said, feeling freer. What if Father's world was just one version? What if I could pick another one?

The fire had already started, and a group of boys and girls were gathered around it, melting the soles of their sneakers on the metal grate. I didn't recognize any of them. Perfect.

"Hey, Lisa," one of the boys called.

"Hey. This is my friend Castley." She pulled me forward, and everyone said their names quickly, like they didn't expect me to remember them. Then Lisa and Emily both joined the circle of girls. I could have joined them, nodded along, but that wasn't enough. Because this wasn't just my first night out; it was also my last.

"Castley?" A boy in a baseball hat stretched around to look at me. "Isn't that a last name?"

I bounced my shoulders. "It is to other people. My father's weird."

He raised his eyebrows and stuck a filter in his mouth. He was rolling tobacco on his knee.

"Are you rolling a cigarette?" I asked, taking the deck chair beside him. The fire crackled, filling the air with hopeful smoke.

"Yeah."

"Can you . . . can you maybe roll me one?"

"Yeah. Sure."

I sat with him for a while, and he told me a lot of boring stuff I never wanted to know about hunting. It was absolutely perfect.

A large group of kids came up the path. I recognized Riva's booming voice, littering the trail with exclamation points, but when she appeared I saw George Gray tailing behind her, and I felt my heart settle. *Fate.*

George didn't notice me at first. I watched him interact with everyone else, teasing and talking in his nonstop, chatty way, like people were fish he was reeling in, and if he paused for breath they might escape.

Someone had brought food, and I got up to get some. I stood directly beside him, and still he didn't notice. Finally I said, "George," until he looked me in the face and tried to figure out if he knew me. "It's Castley."

He walked back two steps. "Oh my gosh! What the heck? What the heck are you doing here?"

"You said I should hang out with your friends," I said.

His eyes fell for a second. "Cool. Awesome. You look freakin' hot. I never realized you had a body." It wasn't exactly the dream compliment, but I still felt a rush of something, dark blood, through my veins. He twitched for a second, like he was working himself around this new information. Then he took my hand. "Hey, why don't you come sit by me?"

Instead of taking me to one of the camping chairs around the fire, he led me off the stage and up into the stands. We sat in the third row, so we could see the fire and everyone on the stage, as if life were a play we were watching.

"I can't believe you're here for this," he said, almost touching his sculpted hair, but stopping himself just in time. He leaned back on his elbows. "You know, it's just kind of a joke. It's not really about the devil or anything."

I swallowed hard. "What do you mean?"

"Don't worry." He stroked my elbow. "It's just something we do for a joke."

"Okay," I said, but all I could think was *devil, devil, devil*. "Sorry. What is it you guys do?" It was cold away from the fire, and my skin popped out in goose pimples.

"Um, at midnight, we just kind of do this jokey little ritual. It's supposed to bring you good luck."

"What kind of ritual?" I tried to swallow my heart. *Real Castley might be afraid of this kind of thing, but Pretend Castley isn't.*

"Well, you see Jaime there?" He pointed at the boy I'd been talking to. "He killed a goat, and at midnight we just sort of stick it into the fire, just for a joke. It's supposed to help us win the Homecoming game."

Why did my night out, my one night out for the rest of my life, have to be a night of amateur devil worship? *Because God wanted it that way.*

"Oh," I said. I couldn't tell if I was scared or not. I had seen scary things. I had seen terrible things. But this was just a joke, George said.

George took my hand. "Are you scared? You look

scared." I couldn't speak. I couldn't even shake my head. The fire on the stage had taken a sinister edge. If I narrowed my eyes, all the figures turned to dark shadows, like demons. "Look, hey. If you don't want . . . I mean, we can just go. You and me can just go somewhere else. This whole thing is kind of lame anyway."

"It's just a joke?" I felt myself saying.

"Yeah. Of course. No one here actually believes that sort of stuff." *I do,* I thought, and then I tried to remind myself that I didn't. Not right then. I was supposed to be pretending. I was supposed to be someone else.

This is it, see? God is punishing you. God is telling you that you can't pretend. That the world is a horrible, devilish place and you need to go home.

I stood up. My arm jerked like a cord, still attached to George Gray. "I think I want to go home. No offense. This just isn't what I wanted it to be."

"Okay." He stood up. "Okay. I'll go with you." I glanced at the stage. "They won't care. Screw them. Let's just go."

"Okay. I need to go get my dress out of Emily's truck." We walked the long way around the stage, giving the others a wide berth so they wouldn't notice us leaving. When we hit the parking lot, we passed a truck with a lumpy blue sheet in the bed, and I swear I smelled the flesh of the rotting goat. *You need to save it.* I had to remind myself it was too late.

It was freezing cold, so cold that I wrapped my dress around me. George Gray touched my shoulder. "Hey? Do you want to wear my jacket?"

I nodded. I wanted to hug him. *Thank you for saving me. Thank you for saving me from that.*

He took his jacket off and dropped it on my shoulders, settling it with his hands. "Where do you want to go?" he said.

I took his hand and pulled him into the woods.

Once we crossed under the trees I felt safe again, I felt like I could breathe again.

"I can't believe they do that," I said.

"Yeah. I know; it's dumb. But it's been a tradition since, like, high school was invented." He tried to keep up with me. I was moving fast.

"And they killed that poor goat?"

"Yeah. I guess in, like, the fifties, they used to slaughter it on the stage. Sorry."

"But why do they do that? Don't they realize that's inviting the spirit of the devil in?" I felt myself blanch. It was the first time I had ever said something religious in front of George Gray, in front of anyone outside my family, and I felt weirdly embarrassed.

"I don't know if they believe in the devil. I mean, not in a real way. They might go to church or get freaked out by exorcism movies, but I don't know. It's not like with you guys."

We reached a small clearing. The moon hung heavy in the sky with the attending stars, eager for their sacrifice.

I turned to face him. "How do you mean, like with us?"

"I don't know." He shrugged in that loose, rubbery way he had. "You guys live like it's still a million years ago. Like you're reliant on God to, I don't know, harvest the crops." He laughed lightly. "People don't think like that anymore, really. They think they can do what they want, and they thank God for letting them. They don't just pray to God and wait for the magic to happen."

"And you think that's what we should be doing?"

"I dunno. But it's a damn sight easier than being at someone else's mercy all day long. Especially someone you can't even see."

"Wow."

"Wow what?"

I took a long breath. "I just can't believe that someone can put so simply something that's been causing me so much . . . turmoil for so long. Where have you been all my life?"

He reached up and snapped a twig in half. "I think sometimes we need other people to see ourselves. I guess."

"Yeah. Maybe we do. Maybe we do need other people."

I moved toward him without thinking. I felt like hope, hope was lifting me, and as I came up I kissed him, soft and then hard, on the mouth. I felt his lips move around mine like two worlds colliding, like dimensions overlapping. *Sometimes you need other people to taste the stars.*

George Gray wanted to walk me home, but I knew that wouldn't be safe, so I walked him home instead. He didn't seem totally comfortable leaving me out in the woods on my own.

"Don't worry," I said as he traced my palm with his finger. "I know these woods like the back of my hand. My brothers and sisters and I, sometimes we spend all night just wandering the woods."

He smirked. "You guys are crazy."

"Gee, thanks," I said, and then I stood on tiptoes and kissed him again. It was weird to think we would see each

190

other tomorrow morning at school. I wondered if we would kiss again or if everything would just return to the way it was, in the light, at school, where we weren't even supposed to talk to each other. *It won't if you don't let it,* I reminded myself. And then I let him go.

He let me borrow his jacket, and I kept it close around me as I walked through the woods alone. I was almost home when I heard a voice call out to me.

"Castella?"

"Caspar?"

Mortimer stepped out from behind the trees. He seemed smaller. I guess because the other boys, like George Gray, were so much bigger.

"How was the fire? Did you get burned?"

"I, um . . ." I touched my lips, worried the lipstick had smudged.

He snorted. "You're worse than Caspar."

"What do you mean, worse than Caspar?"

"We share a mattress. Use your imagination." I had no idea what he was talking about, but I knew it must be something sexual. He started to turn away.

"You're such a hypocrite!"

"I'm not."

"Do I need to pull out a dictionary?" I put my hand to

191

my hair in exasperation and was surprised to find it loose. "I don't understand. I mean, I get that you don't like Michael Endecott, but why are you so disappointed with Caspar, when you did the exact same thing?"

"It wasn't the exact same thing."

"How do you figure?"

"We did it for different reasons."

"Okay," I said. "Why did you kiss Lisa Perez?"

He cocked his head. He had a new expression he'd been wearing lately, that made him look like he was frozen. Cold around the edges. "I wanted to see what it tasted like."

"What *what* tasted like?"

"To be someone else. To be normal. I think you know what I mean," he said, as if he knew about George, as if he knew *everything*.

"And what did it taste like?"

He smirked. "Death."

I kicked the dirt. "Why are you being like this?"

"Because Father is right. Father is right about everything, and one day you'll see, if you haven't already." He gazed into the darkness over my head. "The world is a horrible place. We deserve better."

"But I like the world." I stepped forward. "I like it here.

I think . . ." I almost said "Father's wrong," but I bit my tongue quick.

"You might think that now. You might think it looks nice, on the other side. What is it they say about grass? You might think you could live there, be like everybody else, but you'll learn. We're Cresswells, that's all. Your parents create the world for you; it's the same for everyone. They assign meaning, and everything that happens, happens through their vision. We are victims of our father's vision, and we always will be, wherever we go, whatever we do. You'll see. The world will turn on you, Castley. Just wait. It always does. The world will let you down, and all you'll want to do is go home."

"This is *not you*."

"Yes, it is. You just never knew me."

"I think you're scared."

His eyes narrowed. "When have I ever been scared?"

"I think it scares you, seeing Caspar, seeing me, knowing we could survive in the real world when you don't think you can."

"Lucky for us, I guess, that we'll never have to find out." He folded his arms, and I knew it was my cue to leave, but something kept me there.

"What happened?" I said. "In the hospital?"

"What do you mean?"

"When you broke your collarbone? Why didn't you tell them what Father did to you?"

He fell back, rubbing his collarbone. "It wasn't Father—"

"It had to be."

"It wasn't Father. It was me. I did it. I told the truth."

"I don't believe you."

"It's the truth."

"I don't believe the truth anymore. *There is no truth.* What about Momma? What about her leg? She fell down the stairs. What if he pushed her?" I didn't know why I was saying this, but it was like I couldn't stop. I was wearing somebody else's clothes. I had kissed George Gray. People could see me. People had talked to me.

"He didn't."

"Remember how they used to argue? But they don't anymore; it's like she's dead now."

"She's not dead." He gritted his teeth. "She's attending God's mercy, like we all should be. We all should be more like her."

"But I don't want to be like her! I don't want to wait! I don't want to wait for heaven! I want heaven right now!" My cheek stung as he slapped it. I put my fingers to my face, tried to catch my breath.

"You were getting hysterical," he said. "I had to hit you."

My breath came in short, throaty gasps. Now I *was* getting hysterical. "Like Father hits you? Like he kicked Caspar?"

He shook his head and backed away. "I wasn't trying to hurt you."

"You were trying to control me—that's worse! That's even worse!"

"Stop screaming, Castley. I mean it."

"Or what? Or what?"

"You're going crazy," he said.

"*I KNOW IT!* At least I know it." I started to run in no direction, through the woods so the trees chased me. Bushes scraped my bare legs. Leaves slapped my face. I couldn't think anymore. There was too much to think about. I needed to stop. I needed everything to stop.

The house appeared in front of me, like a wicked, wicked tower. I fell down to my knees.

"Please, please, God. Give me the strength to help myself. Please let me save my family. Every last one of them. Please, God, let me save them. Please, please, please."

And then, as if in answer to my prayer, I heard him scream.

195

twelve

I ran toward the house as his voice broke and dispersed. A pleading quiet followed. A quiet that said, *It never happened, you heard wrong.* But still I ran.

As I vaulted into the kitchen, the overturned bucket cracked. I landed hard on the windowsill. I had to scurry to get in, boots scraping on the wood outside. I heard footsteps upstairs, downstairs—or did I imagine them? As if the house were waking from a deep sleep. The buckets on the floor were all empty, so they didn't splash as I knocked them to the floor.

I ran through the hallway, toward the stairs, toward his bedroom. I saw a dark figure coming down the steps. I screamed.

"Castella Cresswell!" He lurched down toward me and

grabbed my wrist. In the dim light I could see that it was Father, and I tried to take my arm back.

"Don't touch me! Leave me alone!"

"What have you done to your hair? What are you wearing? Where have you been?"

Caspar appeared at the top of the stairs. He was shirtless, and even in the dark I could see his chest had been burned from his neck to his navel. That was why he'd screamed.

"You're a monster!" I screamed at Father, twisting like a wildcat. "I know it was you! I know it was all you when you said it was God!"

He took my shoulders in slow motion, with supreme calmness, and held me against the wall. I kicked out and fought him.

"Let me go, please! Just let me go!" I didn't just mean right then. I meant forever and always. Being trapped seemed like the worst thing in the world. It seemed like the crux of my problem: *I want to go, and Father won't let me.*

"Castella, calm down. You're hysterical. You're not going anywhere."

I threw my weight down, trying to drag myself away. I kicked him between the legs, my own father, because

I'd heard that always worked, but he didn't even flinch. I tried to climb up the wall, but he held me down. He was so strong, so much stronger than I'd ever thought a person could be. And it wasn't fair.

All I wanted was to be free. To run, to run away as fast and as far as I could. But I couldn't. Not tonight. *Not tonight.*

"Father, please," Caspar said.

I went slack in Father's hands, but my mind went faster, faster. *Be good, just for now. Do as you're asked, and tomorrow, or the next day, just when he thinks things are fine and all right, you will run like hell and never look back.*

Father held me there. "Castella Cresswell, where have you been?"

I lifted my head and looked at him, a drowsy smile hanging on my lips. "It's none of your damn business."

He yanked me off the wall so fast my shoulder popped, and then we were walking, moving toward the door.

"Father," Caspar called. "Where are you taking her?"

Father wheeled me around. "Caspar James Cresswell, you will go to your bed right now, or by the wrath of God I will strike you down."

Caspar hovered for a moment, then disappeared into the hall.

And the train kept on rolling.

Father dragged me through the front door and toward the woods. I had fallen into a composed, almost hypnotic state, and I kept up with him without protest.

My eyes traveled over the woods as if they were new to me. White trunks, like twisted bones, and leaves that curled into fists. And the watchful eye of the drowning moon hovered overhead. Why did the world choose that moment to look more beautiful than it ever had? I wanted to cry, but I didn't know if I even could, or would, again.

I observed Father's face as he led me through the trees. His blue eyes were so light, they were almost clear. How could someone so beautiful be so horrible? The forest changed beneath my feet: leaves and roots and trees and colors. I tripped.

Father jerked to a stop. "Tie down your hair," he ordered, releasing my hand.

"Okay." I reached for the hairpins I'd stuffed in Lisa's jean pockets.

I leaned against a tree and put up my hair. I did it

very calmly and slowly. And I wished that when I finished, everything would disappear.

"Where are we going?" I said softly.

"I'm taking you to God's Chambers."

I gasped, then rubbed my throat as if I'd been choked. We couldn't go down there, not now, when all those kids were there. I tried to imagine what would happen if Father and I went storming down the stone steps. If he tried to lock me up under the ground. *They wouldn't let him. They would stop him. And George Gray would rescue me and I would go and live with him and when we were old enough, we would leave Almsrand forever and never come back.*

I finished my hair. "Let's go," I said.

He didn't take my arm. In fact, he seemed confused by what was happening. His pace slackened, and then meandered, as though he were stumbling through a dream. But this was my nightmare.

We passed by the lake without saying a word. I wondered if he was losing his resolution. I felt myself start to think, *Maybe God warned him,* but I put a stop to that fast. *If there is a God, he's not working for your father,* I told myself, and I almost believed it. I could feel the possibility feathering behind my eyes, starting to take shape. *Your father did not create the world.*

It was quiet as we approached the stage. I increased my pace. I wanted to see them there: all my classmates gathered around a fire, like normal people, in a normal world. A world that, maybe, I would one day be a part of.

As we crested the hill at the top of the stands, my heart quickened. The horizon expanded, spilling down into the amphitheater. The open moon flooded the stone space with light.

I gasped, reaching for Father as my knees gave out. The goat was strewn across the stage in pieces. Guts spooled out in red ribbons. Hoofs were scattered like junk. Its head was impaled on a castle turret, gooey black eyes melting into blood.

Father stumbled back, then dropped to the ground at the top of the stands. He put his head in his hands. I thought he might be crying. I forced my eyes away from the stage and sat down beside him.

He stayed like that for a while, just holding his head in his hands like all of this was a message meant just for him.

Then he lifted his head and held his hands out, palms up. "You see, Castella? This is what I protect you from. The world is a wicked place—a carnal, lustful, destructive place. It's not what I want for my children."

I ordered myself to be strong. "What happened to Caspar?"

His eyes flickered like faulty lights. "Your brother is struggling with his carnal urges. This is but another aspect of the flesh which is determined to destroy us."

I took in all the breath I could, and I held on to it, lest I die just by speaking. "What did you do to him?"

He narrowed his eyes and shook his head. *Father.* This was Father. "I did nothing to your brother but go to him when he screamed in the night."

I felt tears form and fall and I clasped my own hand tight.

"Castella, why are you crying?"

"Because I can't tell if you're lying. I can't tell whether you're telling the truth or not. I can't ever tell."

"Faith is a choice, always."

"But I've *seen you do wrong.*" I buried my head in my hands. And I squeezed my eyes so hard that the light came through. Only this time I thought the light came from me.

Faith is a choice. Like Mortimer said Father never broke his collarbone. Like Momma said her leg was just an accident. They all chose to believe in him. We *all* chose to believe in him. I did it all the time. I questioned what

I saw and what I felt. I went crazy putting God everywhere, in everything, because if God wasn't responsible, what did I have? An abusive father and a family living in terror.

Father reached out and rubbed my shoulders. I struggled with the bile rising in my throat. "The flesh is weak, Castella. That's why I'm grateful that our time here is brief. I can see you suffering. See your brothers and sisters. Your mother—"

"Why don't you just get a job?" I spat. "Why don't you just do that? Why can't you just be normal? Then we wouldn't have to suffer so much. We're all starving. We're going to starve to death, and all you do is speak like you think someone is writing everything down!"

He shook his head with his stupid superior wisdom. "God has a different plan for us."

"And we have no say in it? We just have to take whatever God throws at us?"

Father flinched. "You know I would never hurt you. Fathers aren't supposed to have favorites, but they do. Just like God does."

I bristled. "I thought Caspar was your favorite."

"Caspar?" he repeated, like he didn't even know who I was talking about.

I stood up. We were done. The spell was broken. If it

weren't for my brothers and sisters, I think I could have walked away right then.

"God helps those who help themselves," I said, and then I went back through the woods alone.

I was almost home when my feet started to drag. I was overcome with an extreme exhaustion, and eventually I just stopped, out there in the middle of the woods.

I sat down on a rock and tried to think. *Maybe you should just leave, now, while you still can.* But I knew I couldn't leave them: Caspar and Del and Jerusalem, even Hannan and Morty. Even Momma. We all had to get out together. But how could we do that? Was that even possible?

You should just leave, now, my head said. *They'll never go with you.* But my heart said no. And my head said, *Where would you go?* I imagined knocking on George Gray's door. He would smile slowly and rush me inside. We would pack our things into a rucksack, and the next morning, we would run away. I saw us walking together down the highway, into the cerulean blue of the opening morning. I stood up and felt my feet move, my footsteps quickening.

A branch broke behind me. I froze.

"Who's there?" I called, steadying myself on a tree. It

must have been Mortimer, or even Father, returned to punish me.

"Castley. It's me." Caspar came through the trees. He wore a jacket, but he held it folded away from the mark on his skin. The burn shimmered like scales in the moonlight.

"What are you doing out here?" I pulled George Gray's jacket tight around me as if to keep my heart locked inside my chest.

"I followed you," he said. "I wanted to make sure you were okay." He smiled weakly, and I wanted to run to him, to wrap my arms around him. But I couldn't. I wouldn't.

"I'm fine," I said. "I guess God decided to take the night off."

He moved closer to me. His hand rose and pushed my hair back behind my ear. "Your hair is coming apart."

"Oh, I don't care anymore!" I pulled pins out, as quickly as I could, until my hair tumbled down over my shoulders.

Caspar sucked in his breath. "It's like an animal," he purred. He really was struggling with those carnal urges.

He came toward me and wrapped his arms around me and held me out away from him, rocking me back and forth, the way he used to do when we were children afraid. I wanted to bury my head in his chest, but I couldn't. The burn glittered on his skin.

"What happened to you?" I said, fingering the collar of his jean jacket. "Why did you scream?"

Caspar gazed down at his chest, then up again. His eyes had that dull blankness. Cresswell eyes, you might as well call them. We all had them. Eyes that only saw what they wanted to see.

"I was . . ." He cleared his throat. "I was having a dream."

"And it came true?" I snapped, impatient. "Caspar, I want to know what really happened. Please."

"A bad dream. The kind we're not supposed to have."

I groaned. "Can someone just give me a straight answer for once?" He looked dumbly at me. I guess that was a no. "All right. Fine. What did you dream? That we all burned up in fire? That the End is coming because our water pipe burst?"

"I dreamed I was having sex with Amity."

My throat cracked. "Oh."

"I know." His face crinkled like it was a sleazy close call. "It's really bad."

I shook my shoulders, trying to shake off the strange twinge of something like jealousy. "No, it's not really bad. It's not really bad, Caspar. Then what happened?"

"I woke up and my . . . skin was burning."

206

"And who else was there?" I moved closer to him without thinking. "Who else was in the room with you?"

"No one. Just Hannan."

"And Father. Father was there, too."

"No."

"But I saw him coming down the stairs."

"He came up when he heard me scream." I could feel shapes start to shift, the truth reforming in my mind. *Maybe Father wasn't there, see? Maybe it was all just a bad dream.*

I squirmed in Caspar's hands. "Caspar, he must have been there. He was probably in the hallway hiding whatever chemicals he used to do this."

Caspar frowned. "Castley, what are you talking about?"

"Father did this. Father did this to you."

Caspar's features darkened. "Cass."

"Yes, he did, Caspar. It's a chemical burn; it has to be. If we could just Google it, like normal people—"

"Google it?" he repeated, as though I'd suggested something abhorrent. He shook his head as if to clear it. "Castley, I was punished. This is my own fault."

"No. God and our father are not the same person."

Caspar's lips twisted in a funny way. "No, they're not."

"Don't you see, Caspar?" I tried to force myself away from him, but he held on to me, and my heart stuttered inside my chest. "Don't you see this is all him? If we left that house, if we just went and lived like normal people, all this would disappear. All the punishments and the fear and the way every tiny thing feels powerful enough to end the world."

Caspar's breath was ragged, and he held me without seeing me. "No. I don't think it would." It reminded me of what Mortimer said, that we were victims of our father's vision and we always would be, wherever we went, whatever we did.

"It's worth trying, though, isn't it?" I said, squeezing him so he flinched. I loosened my grip, but he wouldn't let go; I think he half liked the pain. "I don't want to live like this anymore. I don't want to live in fear."

Caspar took a deep breath and held me even tighter. "Castley, Castley, what are you going to do? You're not going to leave us?"

"We could all go," I said. "All of us could go together." I gathered my breath. "Caspar, the two of us, we could convince them, together."

"Castella. This is where we belong. We belong together. We're a family." He caught my eyes. "Don't you remember what it was like, when they took us away? We'd all be separated. . . ."

Of course I remembered. Losing my siblings was like losing my whole self, but maybe that was only because there was so little of myself to keep back then. But now I was starting to see things, visions of the world beyond the fence, on the other side of life. How could I make my brother understand that? "Caspar."

"You wouldn't leave us."

I set my jaw. "I wouldn't have to. If Momma—"

"Castley." He reached up and unwound one of my curls with his fingers. "Momma's not . . . Momma's hardly here at all."

I cocked my head, seeing something I had never seen before. Caspar hadn't mentioned God at all.

"Do you still believe it?" I whispered in spite of myself. "Do you still believe that Father's right?"

He took a deep breath, spinning my hair in his fingers. "It's not that," he said. "It's not that I don't believe it. It's just that maybe . . . maybe I wish it weren't true."

I moved to hug him, then stopped just short. But he went the rest of the way for me, holding me against him even as he hissed through his teeth.

Please, God, save Caspar at least.

* * *

The next day outside the drama room, Mrs. Fein had posted the cast list for *Macbeth*. Del and I had been selected as witches, even though we never auditioned. Mrs. Fein came to my desk before class started.

"Did you see the cast list?" she said, like it was a surprise to her, too.

"Yes," I said.

"I know you didn't audition, Castley, but I think you're a terrific actress."

"Sorry. What did you say?"

"I said I think you're terrific."

"No, I mean, you know my name."

Her laugh fluttered out. "I can finally tell you two apart. I think it helps to have you in separate class. With the two of you together, I just think of you as a pair." She cocked her head. "You've really come into your own, you know. Have you thought about drama school?"

It was like she was speaking a foreign language. *"Drama school?"*

"Yes. I think you have a lot of potential."

"You do?" She was probably reconsidering that now. "Yes."

I had never, ever considered going to drama school. When you're living in a fog you don't see clearly, but the clouds were starting to disperse now, maybe. The world was finally opening up. And maybe somewhere, in some possible world, there was a Castley Cresswell who went on living, who went to drama school, who got on the road and kept on walking, to wherever, to wherever a world of endless possibilities took her.

Mrs. Fein put her hands on her hips. "Now, what do you think about the play? You would need to come to rehearsals for forty minutes after school." Father would never approve of that.

"Yeah," I said. "That would be fine."

Mrs. Fein nattered on for a while about costumes, then returned to her desk. George Gray leaned over.

"Hey, congratulations! I'm a palace guard. I wanted to be *you-know-who*, but I think they always pick upper-classmen for the big roles, you know, because they'll never get the chance again and stuff. Oh! I don't mean any offense because you're a junior. I just mean, you know, like, the really big roles . . . Not that yours isn't a big one." He offered a wobbly smile.

"Okay," I said. I tried not to stare at his lips, which looked different in the fluorescent lights. *You kissed those.* I thought about the goat and I wondered if George would have stayed if we hadn't left together. *Of course not.* I almost asked him outright, but the thought twisted in my stomach.

"Hey, so," he said. "Are you going to watch your brother play on Friday? I think he's really gonna nail them, man. You should see him at practice. Your brother is seriously amazing."

Not one single member of my family had ever seen Hannan play. We had never been allowed. "Yeah, definitely. We're definitely going to Homecoming."

thirteen

Delvive corralled me in the lunch line.

"What's all this about the play?" she said, fussing with her hair. "Mrs. Fein said you said yes."

"I did."

"But you know we're not allowed to do that," she said. I also knew that Emily Higgins had been chosen as the third witch. I was pretty sure that was why Del's cheeks were pink and her voice was breathless.

"Forget about Father for a second. Do you want to do the play?"

I watched Del try to forget about Father. I could almost see the mist shifting in her eyes. But it wouldn't disperse. "Castley, you know we're not allowed."

I put a hand on her shoulder. "Just leave it to me."

*　　*　　*

I cornered Father in the hallway before scriptures. Everyone was gathered in the living room. He looked narrowly at me before I even opened my mouth.

"Castella—"

"Father," I interrupted. "Delvive and I have been asked to be in the school play."

"Well," he said in his musical voice, "you're going to have to decline the offer. If you're worried about upsetting anyone, I'd be happy to call your teacher for you."

"No. I'm not going to decline the offer. I want to do it. I don't know if Del does. She can decide for herself." I could see Del in the living room with her head cocked in our direction.

He smiled. I hated how he smiled when he argued with us, like it was all just a game to him. Like we were his little toys, his experiments. "Castella, I will not allow you to participate in a play."

"Okay, Father," I said. Two could play at his game. I wouldn't argue with him. I knew I wouldn't win. But I would go to the play rehearsal after school tomorrow, like everyone else. And if Father wanted to punish me, if Father wanted to lock me in a cave out in the woods, I would threaten to tell on him. Or I *would* tell. I would tell George Gray, and he would come rescue me. He would kiss me through the sewer grate, like Lisa kissed Mortimer, and then I would tell him the lock combination and he would set me free.

I didn't examine this thought closely, because if I did I would have to admit that I wouldn't tell. Not just because I was afraid or because there was no one I could trust, but mostly because of one thing: habit. Habit was the great destroyer. Habit, because I had never told before. Habit, because even though the sands were shifting, it was still just a game, a heady thrill. Habit, because how could you overthrow an old world when you didn't have a new one to take its place?

I flounced into the living room. Father's eyes trailed me as he took his place at the front of the room. I think he knew I had no intention to mind him, but he couldn't argue if I didn't argue first. He was a very careful manipulator, Father. I didn't think I had ever truly appreciated it. But I was his daughter, and I had learned from the best.

I put up my hand. "Before we start," I said, "I have something I want to say."

Caspar caught my eye. I'd heard from George Gray that he and Amity weren't speaking anymore, and all because he actually wanted to have sex with her instead of his own sister.

"This isn't a family meeting, Castella," Father said. "This is scripture study. It's a time for quiet reflection on the word of God."

My eyes drifted over my brothers and sisters. Momma kept her eyes on her lap. *This is for you,* I thought.

"It'll only take a minute." I stood up. "I think we should all go to Hannan's football game." The air seemed to crackle. Hannan's eyes shot up. His message was clear: *Don't you dare make this about me.* I realized Father might just bar Hannan from playing completely, and I felt the first twitter of nerves. "It's just, we've never seen him play, and this is . . . this is the Homecoming game. It's a once in a lifetime experience."

Father's smile twisted. "Thank you, Castella. Can you please begin reading? His Marvelous Plan, sixty-six." He handed me my book.

I did what he asked. I wasn't backing down. As we read, the tension in the room dissipated. But the idea was there, a candle that hadn't been blown out. *Why don't we all go to the Homecoming game? It's a once in a lifetime opportunity.*

That night Del flipped back and forth on her mattress beside me. The scent of dead flowers was strong in our room, and when the wind came through the window, they crackled like scattered applause. After a while, I sat up in bed. Del leapt up straightaway.

"What's all this about?" she said. "The play and the football game and everything?" Baby J was too still on her mattress, so I knew she was listening, too.

I tried to act nonchalant. "Don't you want to do something? Don't you want to be in the play? Don't you want to be in the play with Emily Higgins?"

Delvive squirmed as if repulsed. "When did you get so smooth-tongued?" I knew it wasn't a compliment; we had always been taught that smooth tongues came from the devil.

"I'm just trying to have a normal life, like everyone else does."

"Well, it doesn't seem like that, just so you know," she said, pulling her quilt up to her neck. "It seems like you're trying to attack Father."

"So what if I am?"

Del dropped her quilt and sat ramrod straight. Even Baby J twisted on her mattress.

"You don't mean that," Del said.

"Our father and God are not the same person," I said stiffly. When I'd said it to Caspar, it felt right, but Del virtually hissed.

When she spoke, her voice was so sincere, it made my heart break a little. "Castley, please, reconsider. I think—I don't want to scare you—but I think you may have allowed the devil to enter your soul."

My mind jumped back to the goat. *What if she's right? What if being complicit in that horrible ritual is what's making you act this way now?*

I tried to force those wicked thoughts away. *Wicked, that's what you are.*

I tried to think of a new word, a fresh word, because all the old ones had old meanings. I would need to learn to speak again. I would need to learn everything over from the beginning, if I wanted to change who I was. *Wicked, that's what you are.*

Somehow the old me seemed stronger; she had years and years on the new one.

Please, God, give me strength. But I wasn't even sure what "God" meant anymore. *Please, please, please.*

The next day at school, both Caspar and Hannan were selected for Homecoming Court. Neither of them would participate, of course. They would defer to the runners-up as they had done in past years. I wondered why the school even bothered announcing them at all.

During drama class, George Gray and I made out in an alcove. I felt kind of funny about it at first. I kept thinking about what Del said, about how I was under the influence of the devil. And then I kissed George harder.

Eventually we came up for air. I rested my head on his bony shoulder, and we made spidery shapes with our hands. There was something so comforting in just being close to another human being.

I was wearing his jacket. I hadn't been bold enough to keep Lisa's clothes, but Father didn't know the coat belonged to George. We were always picking up clothes out in the woods, my brothers and sisters and I, so I doubted he even noticed it.

George and I made a steeple with our fingers. "You're so kind of sexy. Especially with your hair down." He reached out with his other hand and poked a finger into one of my braids. "I wish you would wear it down like at the bonfire."

"Okay," I said, swallowing the taste of guilt that seemed to accompany every minor rule break. "Help me take it down."

I removed a pin, and then his hands joined mine, brushing against my bare fingers. I tried to regulate my breathing. It was strange how it made me feel so violated.

No, not violated, I told myself. But I couldn't think of a word that fit.

My heart thumped, and the voice at the back of my head said, *You shouldn't let him do this. Your hair is sacred.* If that was how I felt about my hair, then sex was going to be a huge problem.

"Are you embarrassed?" he cooed.

"No, I was just thinking of something else," I said, before I realized it would be pretty clear what I'd been thinking about.

"Jeez, you use a ton of these." George had the pins collected in one hand.

"I think my sister put in extra this morning to punish me."

"Oh yeah?" He smiled. "Why does she want to punish you?"

I sighed. "Long story. Basically my entire family thinks I'm under the influence of the devil."

George smiled. "Awesome." I tried to hide the way his flippant comment grated. He continued to work, and my hair loosened. I felt the weight of it as it prepared to drop. "Okay, this should be the last one. Dun-duh-da-da-da!" He pulled the pin and my hair fell in one heavy rope. It spilled across my shoulders. George grinned proudly. "Your hair is awesome," he said, and then he kissed me gently on the lips as my hair tumbled down around us.

At lunchtime my brothers and sisters were not happy. I had not put my hair back up.

Caspar watched it like it really was an animal and it might lunge for him at any minute. Hannan offered a backhanded compliment: "Your hair is the prettiest thing about you. You shouldn't just show it to everyone."

Delvive said, "I feel bad for you."

And Mortimer said, "Give it a rest."

But I didn't put my hair back up. Even when my stomach knotted and I felt my toes being licked by invisible flames that said, *Castley, Castley, you're wicked, wicked, wicked.*

It's just hair! I wanted to scream. This was going to be a lot harder than I'd thought.

That night after scripture study, Father held us in place with a lifted hand. He looked exhausted. His face seemed to be coming apart in my mind, separating into unwholesome pieces: the shadows under his eyes, the sweat across his brow, the deep grease in his hair. I had gone to my first play practice that afternoon, and he hadn't even noticed. So much for *God is watching*.

"I've been praying long and hard," he said. "And after speaking to God, I realize that I may have been hasty in my dismissal yesterday. I should not have ignored Castley's vision."

My stomach twisted. He was trying to tie the stupid dream I'd had with my request to go to the Homecoming game. It was just a dream. *But it is a strange coincidence.*

"Friday night, we will all go to the Homecoming game as a family. Except for your mother, who would rather stay at home."

There was a sickening rush of adrenaline in the air, or maybe it was just in me. Caspar put his head down. Delvive glared. I wanted to stick my tongue out at her. *Who's influenced by the devil now, huh? Father says I was right.* Although maybe that wasn't the best recommendation.

I was so thrilled with my progress that I decided to push the boat out a little bit. After school on Friday, I went to speak to my mother.

The headboard of my parents' bed was exquisite. It had angels carved into the wood, cherubs with eyes lifted

222

always toward heaven. But in the last few years, like everything in our house, the wood had broken out in downy white mold. To get rid of the mold, Father bleached the angels. Now they were faded and chalky and splintered.

When I entered the room, my mother sat beneath the bleached angels, reading Father's book of revelations intently. She didn't look up.

I walked carefully to the end of her bed, waiting for her eyes to lift and meet mine. "Momma?" I had taken my hair down at school again, but I put it back up after play rehearsal. I had done it myself, so it looked rushed and messy. Delvive had turned down the part in the play.

I sat down on the trunk at the end of her bed.

Momma turned the page. "Castella, I'm in the middle of reading."

She didn't have time for any of us, except Caspar. She had doted on us as children, but as we grew, she began to look at us like we were strange and irritating creatures. I sometimes thought she might be jealous of us, but maybe that was just a wishful way of making it seem right when it wasn't.

"I just wanted to speak to you for a second," I said, tracing the footboard with my finger.

When I didn't come out with it immediately, she sighed and put her book down in a big show of impatience. What was I even doing there? My plan had been to feel her out, to see if she might be amenable to running away with all of us, to leaving Father alone with his madness. But how would she run away? She couldn't even walk.

"Are you going to the football game with us?" I said, even though I knew the answer. I thought maybe I could charm her with concern. She had ignored me for years, yes, but had I bothered to go to her? Never. I kept quiet because I thought it was the right thing to do.

"No, Castella, I'm not. What do you think? Would you carry me down the stands like a load of junk?" My mother had once had a pretty face; she was delicate like Mortimer and had the same fairy glow that Caspar had. But she was ugly now, as much as it pained me to say it. Her face was hard and pinched. Her eyes were always scowling and suspicious. *That's what you'll look like, too, if you stay with Father.*

"We could. I mean, not like junk, Momma, you're not junk. But Caspar could carry you." I tugged the edge of her quilt. "He would be happy to."

"I don't want to go to a football game." She squeezed the cover of her book. Her deep blue veins bulged beneath the pale shimmer of her skin. "You think I wanna go out there in front of all them horrible people, so they can stare at me and my children? I don't want to see those people. I don't want to see any of those people again! Never again!" She leaned forward in her bed, clenching her fingers into fists. Then she fell back, flinching. Her lips made a crooked smile, and her left eye twitched. "Don't think I don't see you, Castella. Don't think we don't all see you."

My face flushed, and I reminded myself these were just tactics. These were just their tactics, hers and Father's, to make me think they knew something when they didn't. *They didn't know. They couldn't know.*

"Okay, Momma. I hope you're happy." I started to stand, but fell back with a jerk. I saw myself, suddenly, in her. Not in the way I looked on the outside, but inside, where it mattered. She looked like my soul, battered and twisted, afraid to move. And I felt terror grip me, in tight hot fingers around my throat.

"How could I be happy when my children tax me so?" She pressed her fingers into her forehead so they sank into the soft skin. "Mark my words, Castella, this little idea of yours will backfire. Your father has warned me that he fears some portentous event in the air tonight.

Strange that you have visions of flames and invite your own family into your pit. You will not cost me my place in heaven—I have earned it!"

My cheeks burned. My mouth tasted of ash. *She's crazy,* I told myself. *She's completely crazy.*

I forced myself off the trunk and stumbled out of her room, feeling completely off balance. I could hear her shout behind me. "I have earned it! By my life! I have earned it!"

The world seemed to shake, but it didn't make a sound.

I wanted to run. I wanted to run into the woods and never return. What did it matter? There was no way out. Momma would never leave. She would never let go. Heaven was the only thing she was hanging on to.

Tears twisted out of me and I ran. I ran smack into Hannan. I leapt back, half wild. He grabbed my wrist. I felt it twist as he jerked me closer.

"Let me go! It was an accident! Let me go!"

It wasn't just Hannan. I felt other bodies close around me: Delvive and Mortimer and Baby J and even Caspar, looking uneasy.

Hannan pulled my arm up tight behind my back. "Stop!" I pleaded. I could feel all their breaths stealing air, their bodies closing the space. *They're going to kill you,* I thought wildly. I didn't know what I was afraid of anymore. I was just afraid of everything.

"Hannan, let her go," Caspar said.

Hannan released me with a shove. I bounced against the wall. I scanned their five faces. For the first time, I understood what the town people meant when they said we all looked alike. Our features were different, but they all said the same thing. *Cresswell-eyed.* I was surrounded. Backed up against the wall by the brothers and sisters I was supposed to be trying to save.

"What exactly is it you're playing at, Castella?" Hannan said.

"What do you mean?"

"Don't play stupid," Hannan said. Mortimer snorted in approval. "All this shit about the play and the football game."

"Don't you want us to go to your game?"

"No. No, I don't."

I laughed, but it sounded more like a wheeze. My hands were starting to shake and I hid them in my dress. "Then why do you even play?"

"For the same reason I do anything. For the same reason any of us does anything." He motioned to our brothers and sisters. "Because God asks me to. I play football to glorify God."

"Like you ran off with that cheerleader?" He balked like he'd been hit. "And what about you, Mortimer?" I pressed on, trying to ignore how wicked I sounded, how wicked I felt. My nerves were on fire. I was burning up in the flames. "You kissed Lisa Perez inside the Grave, and that's just for starters. And you, Del, whether you're aware of it or not, it's pretty obvious there's something going on between you and Emily."

"How dare you even suggest such a thing, you viper!" She shoved me hard against the wall, but I barely felt it. *They all hate you. All of them. Is this what you wanted? Is this what you want?*

My eyes fell to Jerusalem. "And Baby J, hiding all your paintings. You have a voice and you won't even use it. And you, Caspar." My throat caught, and I swallowed it. "I don't know what you're doing with Amity. But it must be pretty bad if you think you deserve that." My quivering hand indicated the burn that went from his neck to his navel.

"Goat hell!" Hannan said.

"What?" I clenched my eyes shut to keep from fainting.

"I said, *go to hell*," he repeated. "So we made mistakes. Everyone makes mistakes, Castella. We've repented for them. You would do well to do the same."

He stood back, holding his hand out like I was a parable: "The Devil in Action."

"This is exactly what the devil does. He tries to destroy you by creating doubt, chinks in your armor, so you think you don't deserve salvation."

"I am not the devil. I'm your sister. I'm trying to help you," I said, although even I could admit I wasn't doing a good job. I was supposed to be convincing them that Father was dangerous, not attacking them for so-called sins.

"You may think you are," Hannan continued. "But you are under the influence of Satan. You would do well to pray for God's forgiveness."

"Yes, yes," Delvive agreed.

"I haven't done anything wrong!"

Mortimer regarded his nails. "We should lock her up in the Grave," he said drolly. "I think that's what Father would want."

Hannan beamed. "Yes."

"No!" I clutched my chest. I thought my heart would be racing, but it seemed to have stopped completely. "No, you can't. We're going to the football game."

"This is more important," Hannan said. His strong hands closed over my shoulders. He looked me dead in the eyes. "Castley, you may not see it now, but we are trying to help you. You have to trust us."

"No!" I wrenched myself away but met with something solid. I looked up to see Caspar standing over me. *Thank God. Caspar will save me. Caspar will stop this.*

"I'll take her down," he said.

"Yes, I'll go with Caspar!" I said, grabbing his arm enthusiastically.

He took my hand and squeezed it, behind my back where no one would see. "Hannan, you have to leave soon," Caspar said. "I'll take her down. I promise."

Hannan looked uncertain, but no one would dare question Caspar. Caspar, the resurrected. Caspar, the best of all of us.

Hannan agreed, and Caspar led me out of the house with a look of dogged concentration. I smiled at Caspar as we crossed into the woods, but he didn't smile back.

fourteen

Once we were out of view of the house, I tried to pull my hand away. His grip tightened, so I dug my heels in and jerked my hand away.

He continued marching, his pretty face twisted into a scowl.

I forced down the lump in my throat. "Where are we going?"

"What did you say to Momma?" I couldn't tell if his voice was angry or just quiet.

"Nothing." I gasped. "I just asked her if she wanted to go to the football game and she attacked me." I hurried after him. "You know, I'm really tired of being accused of being under the influence of the devil all the time."

Caspar shook his head. "You really shouldn't bother her."

"Thank you for your support."

Caspar shot me a look. "Castella, our mother is a very unhappy person."

"I get that."

"Well, it's not just all about you all the time," he spat. He had never spoken harshly to me before. I wasn't quite sure if he had ever spoken harshly to anyone, apart from himself.

"I wasn't thinking about me!" I said, scurrying along beside him. "I was thinking of everyone. Caspar, don't you see? Our father is crazy. He hurts us. One day he might go so far as to . . . *Anything* could happen—don't you see that? Anything could happen by accident. Or by design. He throws around the word *God* like a weapon, but I don't think he knows the first thing about God. Or anything else. He uses God's name to give himself power."

Caspar pushed through the forest so it sped past in a kaleidoscope of color.

"We need to get out," I said. "All of us do. Now. Before it's too late." My voice sounded weak to my ears.

He spun around to face me. His expression had darkened. "Castella, you know, I don't like to tell anyone what to do. I think a person should be left to make their own mind up. All I can tell you is"—he took a sharp breath—"my own experiences. And I know that lately I've been . . . *confused.*" One of my stars was carved into the tree beside him, and he stuck his finger in it, traced the points. "I started to question things, maybe. I did things I knew were wrong, but I told myself they were right. I realize now that I was allowing the devil to influence my thoughts, because . . . because of something I wanted." I knew he meant Amity. "And I kept trying to justify myself. I tried to convince myself that Father might be wrong, just this once. Or just slightly wrong. I tried to bend the rules. I told myself that it was fate, that it was part of God's plan. But I realize now that was wrong."

"But the other day you said—"

"I said, *I realize now that was wrong.*" He took a deep, dangerous breath. And he looked so dazzling—*God's warrior*—that it would have been easy to cave in, to take his hand and say, *Yes, yes! Dear brother! I was lost but now I'm found!*

He rested his hands lightly on my shoulders. Then, swallowing hard, he drew them down, so his finger pads dragged along my bare skin. "Castella," he said meekly. "You are promised to be my eternal companion. And I really hope that you will choose to live in a way that you might be worthy of it." He reached up and rubbed a lock of my hair between his fingers, watching me with eyes so wide, they were like two holes torn onto a blue sky. *That's what heaven looks like.* I felt it rush through me, gush through me, and I fell against him.

I think I kissed him first, although it happened so stupidly that I can't be sure. But when our lips touched, I felt light everywhere. As if heaven were the taste of his lips, the rush of my blood, and the tightening of something heavy deep inside me. I felt his hard, unyielding body pressed up against me. And I wanted him inside me. I wanted him to crash like a crown over me.

He kissed me like he was trying to fight me off, but it only pushed him deeper, deeper into my soul.

He made a wounded sound and then he pushed himself away, falling back against the trunk of a tree so my star hung over his left shoulder. "I . . ." he gasped, and then he stopped, working his jaw like he'd forgotten how to speak.

Fear gripped me, suddenly, absolutely. I had just kissed my own brother. It was disgusting; it was perfectly disgusting. It was exactly what Father wanted.

"I'm sorry," I said, to no one, to myself. "I'm so sorry."

I lifted my skirt and I ran. Caspar didn't run after me. My heart wanted me to stop, to turn around, to race back, to wrap my arms around him and forget about this world, to wrap my eyes and my heart and my lips around another, better world. *And we'll all be Cresswells together in heaven forever.* But I thought that might be the voice of the devil. I was beginning to wonder if I could tell the difference.

I went to the amphitheater first, without really thinking about it. That was where I was supposed to go, and maybe I thought Caspar might be there. But he wasn't. *You need to go, you need to go now. You need to get away before something bad—something worse—happens.*

Twilight was falling, and the amphitheater was a sterile and sunless blue. I walked around the side of the stage, toward the trapdoor. *Maybe you should go down there. Maybe you should ask for forgiveness and return to them, to him.*

But that would be wrong. *Not wrong, stop saying "wrong" or thinking "wrong." There is no good or evil any-more—how can there be? When everything is good and evil all at once. When everyone believes the opposite so intensely. The devil is nowhere until people put him there.*

I fell to my knees in the mud. I clasped my hands

235

together like two wires trying to catch a current. I lifted them above my head, but nothing caught. The air was dead, barren. The world was cold again. *Just like you wanted it to be.*

You can never go home. It was finally done. The spell was broken. The thing I was most afraid of had finally come true. None of my brothers or sisters wanted me. Not in the right way. They thought I was wicked. They would never leave. *You can just go home. Go home. Keep on pretending, knowing that you're living a lie—*

But my mind stopped there, because I couldn't even do that anymore.

You don't believe it. You've finally admitted it. And it's the worst thing that's ever happened to you.

I left the woods. I went into town. The sky darkened by degrees, like an onion shedding skin. The streets were scattered with people dressed in greens and blues. The school colors. I walked up the main drag, my dress stained with mud and my hair loose and wild. People on the street stared. I wasn't invisible anymore, at the exact moment I wanted to be.

I kept walking until I reached The Chicken Shop. There was a stairwell on the side leading up to an apartment on the second floor. I put my hand on the banister and dragged myself to the top. A sign over the door read HOME SWEET HOME, like even the universe was setting me up.

I didn't snap out of it until I pressed the buzzer. Then I realized what I was doing, too late. I looked like a crazy person, even more so than usual, with my eyes tear-stained and my hair awry and my dress stained with dark mud in two eggs below my knees.

I tried to arrange myself in the side window when the door opened.

"Oh. Hi. Sorry."

A woman stood in front of me with her hand on her hip like she was holding an invisible child—a normal woman in a white T-shirt and jeans. I almost wanted to cry because my mother might have looked like that, she might have been like that, if she'd stayed on the other side of the woods.

"Are you all right?" the woman gasped. "Do you need help? Do you want me to call the police?" As she spoke she surreptitiously pressed the flat of her hand against the screen, as if I might try to force my way inside.

"I'm looking . . . Sorry. I'm actually looking for George. He's my drama partner."

She cocked her head slowly, lips pursed. "George is

downstairs," she finally admitted. "With his friends. They're going to the Homecoming game."

"Okay." I tried to nod encouragingly, but my neck felt stiff. I moved carefully away from her and back down the stairs.

I slunk into the alleyway and tried to fix myself in one of the shop windows. My loose hair had gone from extraordinary to deranged. My face was pale, pinched, starved. I had deep, dark circles under my eyes. *You look like a crazy person.* But George wouldn't care. George would help me. George was a nice person, a good person.

My eyes went straight to him as I passed beneath the door. The bell rang over my head. George sat in the corner with a big group of kids from school. I saw Lisa and Riva and all the girls from that day at the Great American. *You've faced worse than this.* I gritted my teeth. I wasn't going to run, not this time. I had run far enough. I never wanted to run again.

Riva saw me first; she was always looking for me, really, me or someone like me. Her shocked expression turned into a smile as I approached.

"Jesus Christ, it's Carrie-fucking-White!" she said.

One of her friends looked up and laughed. "Oh my God," she snorted. "On fucking point."

Lisa took mental notes, but did nothing, as usual. George looked at his thumbnail.

"Sorry," I said. My voice came out meek and scratchy. I cleared it, adjusted it. "I need to talk to you about something."

"Oh my God, did you get the Cresswell pregnant?!" Riva demanded.

My eyes flitted over her, but I kept my cool. "It's just about our scene."

"Yeah. Okay. Cool." He pulled up his collar and shot his friends a look. They all watched in silence as he followed me out the door.

I led him around the corner, into a lot behind the restaurant. Once we were there, I cried. I knew I shouldn't and that it wouldn't help my case at all, but I couldn't stop the tears. I didn't sob or anything. I just kept completely quiet as my face made a crying shape. So it was like part of me was crying, the dying part, while the rest of me continued on regardless.

"I'm sorry. I didn't mean to bother you, but it's really important."

His face was pale except for two hectic spots on his cheeks that had gone a soupy purple. "Um, Cass? I don't mean to be a dick or anything, but I feel like I should tell

239

you that I don't really want a girlfriend, you know? I mean, I'm just a freshman. I'm not ready for anything serious."

His rejection didn't even sting. I was too numb to feel it. I was trying to tell him that my entire life was collapsing around my ears, and all he cared about, all he could talk about, was how he wasn't ready to hold hands in front of his buddies.

I laughed, but it sounded hard and scary. He moved back, as if I carried some disease. "George, I don't want to be your girlfriend. I just . . . I just need a place to stay."

This only served to aggravate him. He held up his hands, moving backward toward the main drag. "Well you can't stay here." He laughed like it was ridiculous. "You can't stay here with my family. We don't have an extra room, and my mom, my mom's really particular about stuff, you know? She likes everything just so. I don't think she would like some teenage girl living with us. Sorry. But she's kind of crazy like that. I'm not trying to be a jerk or anything. But I really can't help you like that. Sorry."

"Can you stop acting like I'm some kind of virus?" I snapped, hands twitching into fists. "I thought you liked me."

"I do." He rubbed his neck. "I do like you." I could tell this was too much for him. He was too young. He was too weak. He was too spoiled and safe to understand the terror I felt, the terror I'd felt every day. He chuckled, a nervous tic. "But it's not like we can just move in together. I mean, c'mon, Cass. We're teenagers. We live with our parents."

"I can't live with my parents," I said. "So where am I supposed to live?"

He moved away, not just in body but also in spirit, and I wondered why I had ever liked him. He was nothing. He was nice because his life was nice, so it was easy for him. It didn't cost him anything, not the way it cost us, the people who suffered.

"Just go back to your family, Castley. I'm sure it will be fine. Everyone's parents are a little crazy, y'know? We all hate them sometimes. But you belong with your family. I don't want to, y'know, I don't want to mess that up. I don't want to separate you and your family."

I wanted to yell at him. I wanted to tell him this was all his idea, but it wasn't. I knew it wasn't. I had used him, used his words. I had told myself he was there for me so I would have the strength to do what I needed to do. And now I had. And I didn't need him anymore.

"I'm never going back," I said. "But what do you care? I don't need you. Or anybody. I don't need anybody."

For a second his face softened, as if in admiration, and he swayed in my direction. Because that's when they wanted you most, that's when they came for you, when they sensed you were strong enough to live without them.

I turned on my heel and I walked, past the faces of my classmates peering out through the window at me, past the streetlights on Main Street, toward the highway, and into the dark.

As I walked, darkness peeled deeper and deeper over my head, tucking shadows into the cracks in the sky. The highway was deserted apart from the occasional car that whipped by so fast that I felt air speed through me, tearing off another layer.

There is no God out there, I swore at the sky, daring it to prove me wrong. *No God, no one, no one to love or save you. You have to save yourself.*

As I walked, my body grew weaker. It grew weaker so fast that I thought I might actually be dying. Soon I couldn't walk at all and I collapsed on the side of the road, at the edge of the woods, and buried my head in my hands.

Oh Lord, why hast thou forsaken me? I would do anything to believe again, to believe in something beyond the darkness, the empty road that went on forever and ever. *If there isn't any heaven after all, if there's nothing there on the other side, then I wish I were never here at all.*

I lay back on the dirt, feeling sanity drain from me like water with no vessel to contain it. I curled my fingers, and they seemed to disappear. I felt myself floating, kept aloft only by pain.

I don't even exist, I thought. *I'm dead. Maybe I was born dead, only I never realized it 'til now.*

The stars took their places over my head, the same way they always did. I could see my constellation, tied to a chair in the sky.

"Don't fight it," I warned her. "You're better off in chains. Without them, you're just nothing. You're alone. You might as well not exist at all."

If dying didn't absolutely terrify me, I might have ended it all. But death was the only thing that felt real to me. *You could have had heaven. You could have had Caspar. But you had to go and stop believing. Now you can't even find safety in heaven.*

It was this thought that pushed me up, so fast my head spun.

"You can't rely on heaven," I said out loud. And then I pushed myself to my feet, stumbling into the open road.

Because if I didn't have heaven, then this was all I had. All I had was now. Right now.

Two bright lights shot out of the dark, rushing toward me with a mad certainty. *But I won't die. Not yet.*

The truck swerved, barely missing me, then shot past. I caught my breath. I heard the engine slow. The truck pulled to a stop, far ahead of me, out on the road.

"Hey!" a voice called out in the dark. "Hey, Castella!" I didn't recognize the voice, but the voice recognized me.

Michael Endecott poked his head out the window and motioned me over. "What are you doing out here? Get in. Get in. I'll drive you home. Or wherever you need to go."

I stumbled toward him. I was still confused, but I felt lighter somehow. I smiled. I felt free.

fifteen

"What were you doing out there in the dark like that, huh?" He tried to catch my eye. In the dark, driving the truck, he looked like Father. "You could have gotten yourself killed."

I fumbled with my seat belt. "I was trying to see if there is a God."

He grunted, shifted the truck up a gear. "Oh, yeah? And what did you see?"

I blew my breath out. "I don't know. I think maybe there is, but I guess I don't know for sure. And I guess I don't need to know, you know?"

He kept his eyes on the road. "Where do you want me to take you?"

I looked at the clock on the dashboard. "It's almost kickoff," I said. "I better go to the Homecoming game."

He raised his eyebrows.

"My whole family is going, to watch Hannan."

"Oh." He nodded, trying to hide his surprise. "Hey, you wanna know something? Your father was the high school quarterback. I bet you didn't know that." He raised his eyebrows like he thought I might be impressed. "He was the most popular kid at school."

I couldn't help myself. "Then what happened?"

His expression dropped. His mouth groped for a second. He landed on, "We don't always understand the people we love."

I didn't know what to say back, because I didn't think I loved my father. Not anymore. Sometimes love was a spell people put you under to keep you from seeing who they really were.

He exhaled. "No matter what he does, he'll always be my brother."

I sat ramrod straight in my seat. "What?"

"Gabriel. Your father. Someone must have told you I'm your uncle."

"Why didn't *you* tell me?"

"I . . ." He looked uncomfortable. "I thought your brother would have."

246

Caspar? "Which brother?"

"Mortimer. When I . . . I know this was a long time ago, but when I took him to the hospital. It was the first chance I ever had to explain everything."

"What everything?"

"That I'm here for you. All of you. If ever you need . . . *anything.* Do you need anything?"

I wanted his help, but I knew I couldn't take it, not yet. If I walked into the football game with Michael Endecott, his brother, Father would run and take my siblings with him. No, I would have to face Father myself.

I took a deep breath and tried not to look scared. "No. It's just nice to know you're there," I said. "It's nice to know that somebody is. *Family.*"

I hoped God would keep my brothers and sisters safe. But if he didn't, I would.

I heard the crowd as we pulled into the parking lot. Their cheers echoed through the stands, filling the night sky with an atmosphere of unholy spectacle. I climbed out of the truck.

"It's like all the stars are here to watch," I told Michael.

He gave me a funny look. "Hey, listen, are you sure you're okay? You're sure you don't need my help?"

I touched the photograph folded in my pocket. "You're the boy in the picture. The one holding the baby." His face went white, all at once. And I knew he couldn't help me. He was too scared, scared of the past. But I lived in this pit, I knew the real shape of it, and only I could climb out of it. "Thank you," I said.

I shut the door behind me and journeyed through the lot, weaving between cars as quickly as I could. Just outside the gate, I saw Riva and her friends. George Gray was hanging off to the side, talking to Katie Leslie. He shivered when he saw me. *Give me a break, will you?*

"Hey, Cresswell!" Riva called. "Why aren't you wearing white?! Your brothers and sisters are all down there! Are you all gonna perform a baptism at halftime?!"

"Isn't it funny how *I'm* supposed to be the freak when *you all* slaughtered an innocent goat?" I offered Riva my best creepy smile. "I don't know whether I believe in hell, but for you, I'll make an exception." My eyes passed over George Gray. *You, too, buddy.*

She gawped wordlessly as I pushed past. Just as I reached the gate she found her voice and shouted, "Freak!"

I turned to face her, staring into her horrible teenage face. "Riva, Riva, as if I give a fuck what you think." I spun around, whipping my hair behind me so it flicked like flames, and I went through the gates, into the fray, to find my family.

I paused at the top of the stands, preparing to descend into the melee. The entire crowd was spread below me, in stands that reminded me of the amphitheater. *They're here to witness the sacrifice,* I thought, and I shivered.

The game had already started. I could see Hannan out on the field, the powerhouse, and I stopped to admire him. Then my eyes found my family. They were easy to spot. They were all gathered together in the front row, dressed in white. I started to descend.

"Castley! Wait up!"

I turned to see George Gray racing toward me. He stopped in front of me, catching his breath.

"Hey," he said, massaging his chest. "I'm really sorry about earlier, you know? I mean, I know I was kind of a jerk, but you just freaked me out, coming in like that. You know, we all fight with our families, and I don't want to cause a fissure."

I looked at his gawping lips and felt repulsed. *I can't believe I kissed that.* "Don't worry," I said. "You just don't understand. That's all."

And then I left him there. Because that was all I had

to say. That was all I *could* say. He was lucky not to understand, and I hoped he stayed that way.

I marched slowly down the stands, toward my family. I could see them watching the game, eyes flicking nervously, every so often, to check on our father, who stared intensely at the field, as if he controlled the outcome there, too.

I pulled up in the aisle and let my eyes drift over them. All I felt was love. Caspar turned first, and his eyes caught mine. And for the first time I could see in them the fear and desperation that lived there. It was as if my own eyes had been washed clean and I was seeing clearly, at last.

I took the open seat next to Jerusalem.

"Castella," she said in surprise. I took her hand. All of them turned at once. All of their eyes went to Jerusalem, and then to me, but no one said a word. Father only smiled and turned back toward the game. He had his hands clasped out in front of him as if in prayer.

We watched in silence. We watched the other team miss and we watched Hannan score a touchdown. But we never clapped or cheered. Because the game meant nothing; it was just something to do. Another way to steal time from the living in scorecards and battles of good and evil.

I was watching the game when he started to hum. I turned as his head dropped between his arms like a puppet. For a second I thought he was dying and my heart lifted, before the guilt could come rushing in. He began to rock.

The crowd around us quieted first. The silence spread in a circle that grew larger and larger, until the only sound was the boys on the field and Father's terrible hum.

He rocked back and forth on his heels, eyes shut, arms clasped, moving faster and faster. So fast I thought for sure he would fall, snap, go mad, and fall apart.

And then he stopped. The crowd was silent. And he opened his eyes.

"The time is now," he murmured under his breath. And then he stood up. And like the puppets they were, they all stood with him. Except for Caspar and me. Our eyes met in the silent crowd.

Father grabbed Baby J and then Caspar, yanking him to his feet. And then he ran, dragging them up the aisle through the crowd. Mortimer and Delvive stumbled behind, chasing Father up the steps as the crowd oohed and aahed at the boys on the field.

I sprinted after them, taking the steps two at a time. And still I could barely keep up. I saw the ambivalent faces in the crowd, and for once I didn't care, for once I didn't feel angry. I only felt scared.

Nothing else matters, I thought. *Nothing matters but saving them.*

We raced through the parking lot, weaving through cars. I broke into a sweat. My tired legs tripped, but I kept up, I kept up and said nothing, until we reached the truck.

"Come children," Father said. "We must go now. Now is the time. It's not safe for us here." Father's eyes drifted over mine, testing me.

There were people in the parking lot; it wasn't just us. He knew that, too. He couldn't make us go, but he didn't have to. Mortimer and Delvive squeezed into the front seat. I couldn't stop them. I had to go with them, but not all of them.

"Wait!" I said. His lip curled. "We need to go get Hannan! We can't just leave him here!"

"Hannan will come after."

"No. He might not know where to find us." I took Caspar's arm, pulled him away from Father. "Caspar will get him. It's almost halftime, so they'll be going to the locker room. It needs to be Caspar."

Father's eyes flickered, but he knew he could trust Caspar to go. He knew Caspar would come back.

"We can't leave Hannan," I insisted. "We need to go together. *All* of us."

"You're absolutely right," Father said, lifting Jerusalem into the bed of the truck. "Go. Bring him to the house. We'll all be waiting there." Father walked to the other side of the truck.

I squeezed Caspar's hand, so hard I could feel my fingernails digging into his sweaty palm. "Go, Caspar. Go and don't come back."

He cocked his head.

"Don't play dumb with me. You know what I mean. It's not safe for you especially, not when you're so confused. You can't make up your mind, so I'll make your mind up for you. You need to go. Get away from us and decide for yourself what's true."

"Castley. No."

My head darted up as the engine roared to life.

"I need you to go, Caspar, please. I can't trust you to make the right decision. And I can't trust myself not to follow your lead." I released his hand. I stepped back, away from him. "You're the best of us, remember that."

"No." He shook his head. "You always were."

I wanted to run to him, to run away with him, but I forced myself back. I wanted him to escape at least. I wanted

253

Caspar safe at least. "I can do this. Go." I raised my voice. "Just go, Caspar! Go now. Hurry, before it's too late." I climbed into the bed of the truck with Jerusalem, wrapping my arms around her. "Hurry! Before it's too late!"

Caspar bit his lip, deliberating. I knew he didn't want to leave us, even for a moment. And I knew that he wouldn't run, he wouldn't escape, even though I wanted him to. He would come back for us. I knew I couldn't stop him.

And I smiled. And he nodded, fists clenched at his side like God's last and only warrior. All I had to do was hold Father off for a little while, and then Caspar would come and rescue us.

I held Jerusalem tighter as the truck started to move and Caspar turned and raced into the dark.

I held on to the straps in the back of the truck as it rocked down the road. Baby J clung tightly to me, whimpering softly.

"We're gonna be okay, aren't we, Castley?" Her voice was scratchy, marred and almost dusty with disuse. She was speaking again. It wasn't too late for her. It wasn't too late for any of us. "You're not scared of heaven, are you?"

"No," I said, stroking her hair. "I'm not scared."

And I thought maybe I wasn't, until we missed the turn to our house. "Move up a second," I ordered Jerusalem. She moved and I leaned forward, knocking on the back window. Delvive opened it for me. Her face was pale as paper.

"Where are we going?" I tried to swallow the fear rising like a balloon up the back of my throat, expanding inside my head until it seemed to press against the back of my eyes. "I thought we were going home? You told Caspar to go home."

"I will go and collect Caspar myself," Father said. "It isn't safe for you there."

"Where are you taking us?"

"I'm taking you to God's Chambers." He kept his eyes straight ahead, so I could only see the back of his head, thrown into dark relief by the headlights. "From there," he said pleasantly, "we will journey directly to heaven. And all of this will be over."

I choked on a jagged breath. I felt my muscles go limp, but I clung to Baby J, holding her tight to my chest as she shivered in my hands.

As we pulled up in the lot beneath the amphitheater, I knew this was my chance to run. I could drop Baby J's hand and sprint toward the woods. I had a feeling Father would let me go, lest he lose the others, but I didn't run. I held tighter to my sister's hand. Because family is the most important thing in the world, and I was going to save mine.

We followed Father up the pathway and into the amphitheater. We walked in age order, like we'd been taught to.

If you don't find a way out, this may be the last place you walk on this earth.

I counted the stars as we passed. *One, two, three, four, five*—and I lost count. Then I looked at the sky. *Maybe tonight you'll be carving stars in heaven. Maybe, instead of gashes on a tree, you'll be making scars in eternity.*

I felt hollow, encased in panic, as we reached the stone steps of the amphitheater. We followed Father to the trapdoor, and we watched as he bent down to unlock it. Baby J took my hand again, and Delvive took the other one.

We stood back as Father opened the Grave. "Go down inside and wait. I'll come back with the others."

I tried to catch his eye, but he had gone very far away. He was chewing the air with a nervous insistence, like a rat chewing an electric cable. His eyes had this kind of stunned hypnotism and I knew I couldn't beat him. I couldn't beat him because he believed in all this. It was as real to him as it was a lie to me.

Mortimer slid down into the opening; he had done it a dozen times before. It was a narrow chute, stony and claustrophobic. I could tell that neither Del nor Jerusalem was eager to go, so I stepped forward.

"Thank you, Father," I said, sitting down and sliding into the chute. My feet dangled in the air and I shut my eyes, trusting in the ground, whatever ground there was, to catch me. I dropped, then slid through the passage, trying to ignore the thought that I was burying myself alive. *We're going to get out of here,* I thought, but it was tough to believe underground, in a cave so dark I couldn't see my own fingers.

Something hissed and light opened inside the cave. I had meant to wait for Jerusalem, to make sure she got down safe, but when the light washed the walls I completely forgot myself.

The walls were covered with wild paintings, drawn in a red paint that looked like blood: bodiless heads, stars, and monsters with wild faces and arms and teeth.

"Who painted these?" I asked Mortimer.

He shrugged. "God."

Limbs in a pile. Men with their arms bound and swords in their shoulders. Children drenched in blood. *This is what it's like inside Father's mind.*

Del came down next and she helped Jerusalem into the cave. Jerusalem seemed the most shocked by the violent works of art. Her eyes widened and she clung to Delvive's white dress. We all jumped as the door shut over us, except for Mortimer, who sat down in the corner and made himself at home.

The floor was slanted, so the ceiling was close or far depending on where you stood. It was bare except for the gas lamp and a wooden trunk tucked into the farthest, darkest corner.

I wanted to take Jerusalem's hand again, but I reminded myself to be strong and held my own dress instead. "What is that?" I indicated the trunk.

Mortimer's head jerked. "I don't know. It's locked."

I moved toward it. "Have you never tried to open it?"

"Don't, Castley," he warned.

"Why not?"

"It's cursed. Father says if you open it, you'll die instantly." He was serious. He had never opened it. He had never looked inside. He still believed in magic, even the black kind. "Just sit down. Wait for Father."

"Wait for what?" My voice echoed in the cave, so the ceiling seemed to shiver. Baby J clung tighter to Delvive. "Wait to die?"

Jerusalem whimpered.

"Castley, stop that," Del scolded.

"Sorry, Del—do you know of another way to heaven?"

Delvive stroked down Jerusalem's hair. "Stop that, Cass, you're scaring Jerusalem."

"She should be scared! We should all be scared shitless right now!" I looked at Mortimer, who looked away. "Is this what you want, huh? What is it you said? 'Her kiss tasted like death'? Well, you're in luck, buddy, because that was just foreplay."

"I don't care," he grunted. When he turned toward me his eyes were shining.

"You want to die?"

"Why not?" He shrugged like it was something fun to do on the weekend. He lifted his sneaker and started scraping mud out of the crevices in the rubber.

"But . . ." I looked at Delvive.

She shrugged as if shoving my eyes away. "Heaven is supposed to be better."

"What if it isn't?" They looked at each other nervously. "What if it's worse and you can't come back?"

"Nice one, Castley," Mortimer shot back. "You know, that's basically sacrilege."

"Father says it is better," Delvive pointed out.

"Father says a lot of stupid stuff."

Delvive sucked in her breath, and Baby J's eyes practically popped out of her head.

"Don't you think it's *convenient* that God wants us now, before any of us can turn eighteen and leave the house? Or how we're all destined to marry each other, so we can never get close to anyone else? Or how he never told us that Michael Endecott is our uncle?"

Mortimer dropped his foot and sat up. "That's not true! That's a lie!"

"You knew," I said. "He told you. That's why you lit that fire, why you were so angry Caspar was spending time with Amity. You were afraid he'd find out that you've been lying all this time."

"It's bullshit. He made it up to trick us."

"Why would he do that? How could it possibly be of any benefit to him to be our uncle?"

"He's an agent of the devil," Mortimer recited without feeling. "He wants to tear our family apart."

"Do you honestly think that the world and everyone

in it is a test rigged for our advancement? Don't you think that's incredibly self-centered?"

"No." Mortimer smirked.

"If you knew he was our uncle, why didn't you tell us?"

He scraped his fingers through his hair, betraying his agitation. "Maybe I don't want to live like everyone else. Maybe I don't want to be Michael Endecott's nephew. Maybe I really do want to die." His eyes met mine and the light seemed to dim.

"But why?"

"Why not?" He bent forward again, pulling his shoe close, and he continued to pick mud from the crevices.

The cursed trunk was in the corner, hemmed in shadows. It had been there all along, but no one dared to look inside. Until now.

I wandered toward the sewer grate, watching the weird way the night sky hid behind the trees. The sick shadows split through the cracks. The sky, with its multitude of stars, was bigger than everything and yet it kept its distance, its intentions hidden. *Why not?* I thought. *Why not live?*

"Oh my God!" I put my hand to my mouth.

"Don't say, Oh my *you-know-what*," Mortimer warned, getting to his feet.

"There's someone out there." I pointed through the grate. I backed toward the shadows and the ceiling lowered over me.

Mortimer peered carefully through the grate. "Where?"

"I saw their foot, their shoes. It was a kind of pink sandal thing." I described a shoe I'd seen Lisa wearing.

The ceiling scraped the crown of my head and I hunched my shoulders. I could see Del and Jerusalem painted into a corner, clinging to the creased fabric of their blended dresses.

"A pink sandal?" Mortimer breathed, hooking his fingers through the grate and pulling himself onto tiptoe.

I folded down in the dirt. With my hands behind my back, I slid my fingers around the rusty metal of the combination lock on the trunk. I turned around.

The number seven, three times. At least Father was consistent. The lock jerked open with a click and I twisted it, slid the bar from the handle. I placed my hands on either corner, and threw back the lid.

I couldn't stop the gasp that escaped my lips. Couldn't, because even in my wildest, darkest dreams, I never could have imagined it. There were long thin objects, smooth and white like bones. Because they were bones—tiny child bones—meticulously bleached white, probably with a bottle of Palmer's Bathroom Bleach.

They were Caspar's bones. My eldest brother, in a pile, in pieces, and laid between the pieces was something thin and silver—the weapon that would see us join him in the afterlife.

sixteen

"Castley, how could you?" Mortimer made to move toward me, but stopped, held by some spell.

I reached into the bones and lifted the rifle. It was heavy in my hands—deadweight—and I used both quivering hands to grip it, turn around, and aim the barrel at my brother.

My heart was throbbing inside my skull. I forgot how low the ceiling was and knocked my head.

"This is what you wanted, right, little brother?" My hands shook like crazy. The gun was heavy, heavier than I had ever imagined a gun would be. It felt fake and real at the same time, like the whole world was colliding on one insane point.

Mortimer jumped back. "Jeez, Castley! Don't mess

around! You don't know what you're doing. You might set it off by accident."

"I thought that was what you wanted?" I watched the muzzle of the gun dance and seem to flicker. What if it did go off? What if it went off and I shot Mortimer? I pointed the gun at the floor, but it wouldn't stop shaking.

"If it's all the same to you, I'd rather leave it to someone with a little better aim," Mortimer joked, but his voice shook. He was scared, scared to die. That was all I wanted to prove. *Put the gun down.*

The gun felt alive in my hands, as if it had always been there, just waiting. The gun was fear, and I held it in my hands.

I pulled the trigger. Before me, some of Father's paintings blew apart, opening up a hole in the dirt that circled, wider and wider, piling in a pyramid on the ground.

"What the hell are you doing?" Mortimer said

"I'm g-going to get r-r-rid of every b-bullet." My voice popped like bubbles. I regripped the gun and shot again.

The hole in the wall blew apart. What was it Father used to say? That God's Chambers led directly to heaven. I imagined the wall crumbling, heaven opening up behind it, like the whole world was just an illusion. Like I could blow it all away.

"Castley! Stop, you fucking idiot! A bullet might ricochet! You might cause an avalanche and bury us alive."

My heart hiccoughed. I tottered toward the entrance, as if in a dream. The gun seemed lighter now. It lifted in my hands, floating toward the ceiling. *This is the right thing,* my mind said. *The right thing, but it feels wrong.*

Del and Jerusalem cowered in the corner. For people who were so keen to die, they certainly didn't show much enthusiasm for destruction.

I climbed into the chute. Dirt shifted under me. There was no solid ground. I planted my elbows deep and aimed at the trapdoor.

"Castley! If that bullet ricochets you're gonna fucking shoot yourself!"

The world exploded, piling on my shoulders in warm dirt. It burned my eyes, tasted dry in my mouth, buried my hands.

"You idiot! You fucking idiot!" Mortimer's hand gripped my shoulder as he pulled me up. The dirt followed, filling the space I'd left behind. He extracted the gun from my sweaty fingers. "Look what you've done."

I blinked, dazed, at the dirt running through the chute.

The passage was gone. There was no way out. I had buried us alive.

"Oh my God," Delvive cursed.

"It's okay!" I cried. "We can just dig. We can dig our way out." I threw myself into the dirt, shoveling it like a dog, but more came, filling any space I created.

"The whole ceiling is going to come down!" Mortimer wrapped both arms around me and dragged me across the cave. He dropped me in the corner like a doll.

I could feel my lungs collapsing, expanding and collapsing. Surely it was all too much. Surely at some point it was all just too much.

"I don't want to die!" I clung to the tail of Mortimer's shirt, pressed the filmy fabric to my face. "Please! I just want to get out of here. I don't want to die!"

He put his arms around me, rocking me gently back and forth. "Well, you sure don't act like it. Jeez, Castley, you nearly killed us all."

"But that's what you want. That's what you all want. Isn't that what you want?" I gazed up at his face. I could see how alive he was, as if he never had been before. His heart raced in the strands beneath his skin, through his nerves. His blood pumped hot into his cheeks.

The chute was flooded. The trapdoor was blocked. But

even though I knew there was no way out, being in my brother's arms made me feel safer than I ever had before.

The clock was ticking somewhere, but under the ground, time had stopped. Once it was clear that I wasn't about to go for the gun, Del and Jerusalem sat down beside us. We linked hands, not all at once, but gradually, so I didn't notice it until it had already happened.

"There are bones in there," I said.

"What?"

I got to my feet, letting go of their hands. I went back to the trunk. The bones were there, exactly as they'd been before, exactly as they'd been for over a decade. I took a deep breath, reached in, and lifted out my older brother's skull. *It's not real,* I started to tell myself, but then I put a stop to that. "It is real," I said out loud. "Everything is real." I lifted the skull into the light so they could see it.

Mortimer's skin went transparent. Baby J cried out and clung to Delvive.

"What is it?" Delvive asked. There was strength in her face, and for once it was like looking in a mirror.

"It's Caspar. The real Caspar."

"But if he was resurrected—"

"He would have kept his body with him." I put the

skull down. I tried to be careful, but it dropped, rattling the bones in the trunk.

"It could be . . ." Mortimer started but didn't finish.

"There's something else. Something I didn't show you." I reached into my pocket and pulled out the photograph. I unfolded it. The creases converged over the baby's head like crosshairs. I handed it to Mortimer first.

His expression tightened, like he was trying to change what he saw. "What is this?"

Delvive slid closer, pulling Baby J. "That's Father," Del said.

"And that's Momma. And that's Michael Endecott," I explained. "And that's Caspar."

Mortimer handed back the picture. "What happened?"

"That's what I said."

"I don't understand how he could look so different."

I hadn't understood it, either. But suddenly, in the dark of the cave, in the dark of the night, I did.

"He chose to," I said. "He was one way, and then he decided to change. I mean, look at him." I held the picture out, because I didn't think it was fair the way they'd stopped looking when it got hard. "I mean, he had it all. They were beautiful, both of them. Michael said Father was the most popular boy at school."

Mortimer snorted. "I can't imagine that."

"He could have gone on to something better. He could have been anything, but he chose this. He chose this, but we don't have to."

"It's already been chosen for us," Mortimer maintained.

"No, don't you see? This picture proves that's not true." I took Mortimer's hand, because I felt something blossoming so strongly inside me that I needed the space, I needed it to grow in his heart, too. "You can be anything you want to be. You can be a corpse, if you want to. Or you can be something else, something you can't even imagine yet because no one ever gave you the freedom. You don't even know who you are yet, so how can you die? You have to exist first, and you can do that, Mortimer. *You can exist.*" We locked eyes and something passed between us, something full, deeper than blood. "Morty, you know this place better than any of us." I scanned the caverns lost in darkness. "Is there another way out?"

Mortimer took a deep breath and shook his head. "No."

"What if we shot the sewer grate?"

Mortimer rolled his eyes. "It's metal. The bullet would ricochet. It could cause another avalanche."

270

"Okay. What do you suggest we do?"

"Pray," Mortimer said.

I think he might have been joking, but Jerusalem moved in closer. "Yes, let's pray. Let's pray and maybe God will get us out."

My heart swelled. I wanted to explain to her that God didn't work that way, that Father was wrong about that especially, but instead I raised my hands and crawled into a kneel. The others fell in beside me.

"Who wants to do it?" Del said.

"I will," I offered. The gas lamp flickered, so the paintings seemed to spark. The air felt heavy, thick. When I shut my eyes, I thought I could hear our breaths push through the grate, out and away, dispersing amongst the stars. "Dear God, first of all we want to thank you for all that you've given us. We want to thank you for giving us one another, so that even when things are bad—I mean, really, really bad—we still have one another, and that makes us feel safe. We want to thank you for giving us brains to think and bodies to act. I know you help those who help themselves, and we're ready to help ourselves, to use our brains and bodies to get ourselves out. Amen."

Mortimer gave me a look as if to say, *What kind of prayer was that?* But he didn't complain.

The light twitched. The lamp squeaked.

"What are we going to do?" Del asked.

My hands had stopped shaking. I coiled them deeper, tightening my fingers. "We have to wait. We have to wait for Father."

We heard everything inside the cave. Every hoot and howl and nighttime sound. Beneath the ground, the whole world rose up like a phantom planet.

Hours must have passed, but I felt no hurry. Only a rising dread, the concentrated Great Unknown. He was coming. What would we do when he came? What would *he* do? What if we didn't, couldn't escape? What if it was too late? What did the End look like? What did it feel like to die?

The only thought I could cling to was Caspar. Not that Caspar would help us escape, but that Caspar was safe. He must be. Unless he'd gone to the house. Unless that was what kept them, as time froze and fled.

Maybe he went to the police. Maybe they drove him to the house. Maybe they stopped Father and soon they will come find us, soon they will rescue us. Maybe.

We heard the hum of a car engine as it pulled into the lot below the amphitheater. We pressed our heads to the wall so it hummed through us. We heard the doors slam. Feet marched up the trail toward us.

"How many?" I said.

Dirt scattered as Mortimer pressed his ear harder. His lips dangled open.

"What is it?" I breathed.

"Nothing. It's just . . . I don't think Momma is with them." He was right. I didn't hear the rattle of her chair or the groans she made when carried.

My breath held itself. My muscles tightened in a noose around my throat. Their footsteps were like a clock ticking on the end of the world.

Then they were over us. Knees in the dirt. The lock rattled, then clicked. The dirt from the chute fanned softly as the trapdoor opened.

"Children?" I shivered at the sound of Father's voice. "What's happened? Are you down there?" My eyes found Mortimer's. Life still pulsed there. Perhaps we shouldn't have waited for Father. Maybe we were safer on our own. If we kept quiet, he might disappear. If we didn't speak, he might go away. He might think God had come for us early. "Hannan, start digging."

My heart twisted. Caspar wasn't there.

The dirt started to pour down, inching across the

ground until it spread beneath our toes. He was going to find us. He was going to keep digging until he found us, killed us, so he could bleach our perfect child bones.

"Father!" I called. "Where's Caspar? Is Caspar with you?"

The earth fell away, opened up for him. The first shard of moonlight struck the back wall of the cave.

Mortimer raised the gun. I shivered, but he gripped my elbow and put the gun in my hand.

I shook my head. "I don't want this."

I tried to push it back, but he forced it away. "Please, Castley. You're the only one. You're the only one strong enough to use it."

The full effect of his words hit me. He wanted me to kill our father. He wanted me to kill Father.

"No!" I hissed. "I can't! You can't mean—"

"Castley, he's a murderer. He's going to kill us; you said it yourself. He killed Caspar." At first I thought he meant my Caspar and I went cold all over. But that Caspar, the Caspar hidden in the ground, was my brother, too. Maybe he had done wrong and Father had locked him down here to do his penance. Maybe he died down here. And when Father found his dead body, instead of mourning him, he told himself a story, a story that

274

explained away life without culpability, about God and resurrection.

A black hole opened in the earth. It grew, wider and wider in a circle, crowned by white fingers. The digging stopped.

A dirty sneaker kicked through the opening. Hannan slid down into the cave. When he saw us, his mouth dropped open. We were cowering in the far corner, under one of Father's horrific paintings. I had the rifle pointed, and Mortimer's hand was keeping it steady.

Move, Morty mouthed as the earth shivered behind him. But instead of moving away, Hannan stepped forward.

"Father, wait!" He held his arms out, moving closer. "Go back! Don't come down!"

Father's sneakered foot appeared, swayed like a pendulum, then disappeared. "What is it, my son?"

"Hannan, get out of the way," Mortimer growled. "Stop protecting him."

"He wants to kill us, Hannan," Del piped in. "He wants to kill us all."

"Caspar's bones are down here. Caspar, our older brother, locked away in a trunk like old junk."

Hannan shook his head. His eyes seemed loose, so

they rattled in their pits. He was still wearing his football uniform, and it was smeared with mud, but it smelled of blood. "It's the devil," he said. "You've fallen under the devil's influence. Like she did."

"Hannan, I'm not—" I started.

"Not you." He wiped his eyes, leaving behind a wide streak of something dark. "Momma."

The gun went limp. Mortimer had dropped his hand. I felt my fingers, the dirt in my nails, the weight, the terrible weight of the gun. "Hannan, where is she? What happened?"

"Hannan, what's happening down there?" Father's voice seemed to come from miles, light-years, away. "I'm coming down."

"They have a gun!" He scraped his hair from his face and staggered toward us.

"Where is Momma, Hannan? What happened?"

"She's gone to a better place."

My heart dropped through me. And inside my skull another heart grew and started banging madly.

"What about Caspar, where's Caspar?"

"She's with Caspar now." He stumbled and put his hands out, trying to catch his balance on thinning air. He staggered, so close I could feel his breath.

The gun was so heavy. Hannan's eyes were so dark.

"Castley, don't let go!" Mortimer screamed as Hannan collapsed over us.

Hannan's fingers worked through mine, tightening around the barrel. And I didn't fight it. I let go. Caspar was gone.

I had asked God for one thing and one thing only. *Save Caspar at least.* And God couldn't even do that.

I tried to catch my breath, but I had no breath to catch. I couldn't move without my brother. I couldn't do anything. I sunk to the floor. I clenched my fists in the dirt, feeling sand slip through my fingers, faster and faster the harder I tried to hold on to it.

I shut my eyes and saw Caspar standing there, as clear as anything. I wondered if that was what God was, something you believed in because you had to. And what would the God in Caspar say? What would the God in Caspar tell me to do?

I knew I was supposed to give up then. That was what a normal person would have done. But I wasn't a normal person. All of my life I had been preparing for this exact moment, the moment when I lost everything. All the things I had been through, all the things my father put me through, had been leading up to this point. And although I wasn't grateful for those things, and although I wouldn't have chosen them, I still knew my own strength because of them. Because what I had been through hadn't made me stronger. That wasn't how it worked. What I had been through had made me realize how strong I already was.

The shell of me cracked, and a new me took its place. A me that was rock-solid, stronger than I could ever imagine. A me who could do anything. A me who was completely without fear. And the crazy thing was, she had been there all along. She felt more familiar to me than any of my previous selves. She was the real me.

With the gun gripped grimly in two hands, Hannan lurched back toward the chute. "It's all right now, Father. Safe."

Mortimer crouched forward. His hand was at my knee, squeezing so tight my reflexes kicked. His feet slipped in the dirt. His ankles arched.

"Morty, don't!" I yelled as he catapulted himself toward Hannan.

The gun went off, echoing through God's Chambers. For a moment Mortimer's image seemed to hang, as if pinned there, a white specimen. Then it crumpled to the floor.

"Oh my God," he said. Blood spread in a circle, bigger and bigger, soaking the white fabric of his T-shirt.

Hannan fell. "What have I done?"

I put my hand in the dirt to force myself to my feet. My head swayed, heavy with the new heart that grew there. Hannan stiffened. I saw him through the vines of my hair. He pointed the gun. I saw its black lips.

Then he cocked it back, opened his mouth, and kissed the muzzle.

"Hannan, no!"

The gun clicked. Smoke poured from his lips. But he was still there. By some miracle, he was still there.

It's out of bullets.

I raced to Morty. "Are you okay?"

"Do I look like I'm okay?" he spat, clutching his shoulder.

"We need to make a tourniquet." I tore the hem of my dress and wrapped it around his shoulder as Mortimer screamed in protest.

The earth trembled, then shifted. Father was climbing down the chute. He appeared, unfolded himself. His face was a paper ghost. His eyes had that Cresswell haze, the one I recognized from a million bad days, the one that screamed *childhood*.

"We need to get Morty to a hospital!" I screamed. I

thought that if I screamed loud enough, if I really screamed, he might hear me.

Father put his hand on Hannan's shoulder, bent down, and scooped up the gun. "You see, it is time. This is what we saw; this is what I saw. This is how it happens. This is God's will." He held the gun up in front of his face, like he wasn't sure if it was there. He traced the barrel with his finger.

I felt Del and Jerusalem on either side of me. I moved to stand. "It's not time. God wants his name back. You've used it long enough."

"For once, Castella, you can go first." Father lifted the gun. He looked almost beautiful, surrounded by the dark swirls of his own mad vision. I saw him like that, beautiful, for the last time. I shut my eyes and felt the air rush past me, through me. There was nothing, nothing left.

"Of course I had to get the last fucking bullet," Mortimer said, coughing, clinging to my skirts.

"We're taking our brother to a hospital," I said, bending down to help lift him. "Come on, Del, Jerusalem. Get him to his feet. Get him out of here." They started to move, walking Mortimer across the floor.

Father blinked at the gun, then held it like a club. "If you take him to the hospital, Hannan will go to jail."

"I'm more than happy to say you did it," I said. Father moved in a flash of white, the beating wings of a dove. Pain exploded across my cheek. I was on my knees in the dirt, and he was coming toward me again. Del and Jerusalem froze. "Get out of here!" I screamed at them. "Please! For Morty's sake!" Mortimer moaned as they moved again.

I scurried on my hands and knees toward the darkest corner, toward the trunk. Father stalked after me. *The bones, I'll take the bones, I'll take the bones and give him what he deserves. The bones and he will get what he deserves* . . . He lifted the gun over my head in the shape of someone righteous.

"May God give me strength," he said. I reached into the trunk.

Crack. Little stars appeared everywhere, decorating the bloodred walls of the cave.

"What did you do?" Father said.

I lowered the cracked remains of my brother's skull. I had used him as a shield. Father backed away in horror.

"What is that?" Hannan asked.

Father's head jerked.

"Don't you recognize your own brother?" I said, laying the pieces down in front of me.

"Brother?" Hannan repeated.

"Caspar," I said. "The first Caspar. The Caspar he killed."

Father backed away in confusion, the rifle dangling by his side. "I didn't—"

"You bleached his bones," I yelled. "Why? Why did you do it? Why did you kill him? Why did you bury him? Why did you try to bury us? We could have had everything. We could have had a normal life—what did you want?"

"More," my father said weakly. The glass had broken, temporarily; there was something living inside it. Something so small, it practically didn't exist anymore. He shrugged. "I just wanted more."

"You killed Caspar?" Hannan said. His face was strange. I couldn't figure out why, but then I realized it was the first time I had ever seen his face register emotion. "You killed my older brother?"

Hannan moved, the way they said he moved on the football field: like everything had been preordained. He wrenched the gun from Father's grasp. Hannan was physically bigger than Father, and Father backed away, cowering, as he closed in.

"You shot your own brother!" Father cried. "You watched me kill your mother! This is the work! This is our holy work! The earth has grown too old for us! We

282

belong together in heaven! Bound together in heaven forever!"

"Somehow I don't quite think you're going to make it." I vaulted from the ground. Mortimer was right; I was the only one strong enough to do it. I moved quickly, lifting the gun from Hannan's fingers. My hair flicked in pale flames as I whirled to face Father.

"Silly girl." His back hit the wall. "The magazine's empty."

I tutted. "Now, Father. I thought you had more faith than that." I slid my fingers along the barrel. "If I ask God to give me another bullet, do you think he would do it?" I pointed the gun at his temple.

Father's lips jerked. His jaw twitched. A thick line of sweat coalesced along his brow.

I looked at Hannan and nudged the gun toward the door. *Hurry up.* He went to Mortimer, helped the girls lift him up the chute.

"Do you think if I have faith, enough faith, God would make a bullet appear?"

Father watched the gun with a manic intensity.

"Do you think God would do that?" The last sneakered foot disappeared. I backed toward the chute and took aim. "Do you think God would do that for me?"

seventeen

The gun didn't have bullets—of course it didn't—but sometimes you didn't need bullets. You just needed faith.

My feet moved so fast, the ground swirled in my eyes. The woods raced by, away from me.

When I reached the parking lot, Hannan, Del, Baby J, and Morty had already piled into the truck. They sat with their eyes pointed forward, as if willing it to move.

"There's no key!" Del called. "There's no key! And Morty's starting to pass out!"

"Shit." I skidded to a stop. My eyes hooked Hannan's.

The keys were with Father.

"I need to go back."

He climbed forward. "Wait. I'll go with you."

"No. Stay with Morty. See if you can hot-wire the truck. We locked him down there. He won't be able to hurt me." I think he knew that I didn't trust him, but it was more than that. I didn't trust anyone. Not even myself.

I walked up the steps to the amphitheater alone. It was the middle of the night. Somewhere far away, my fellow teenagers were probably asleep, dreaming in their beds. For once, I didn't want to be them. I was awake now. I was different, but not in the way he said I was. I was special, but not because he made me.

The path was long and my feet were heavy. The trees opened up as I crested the hill, so in a way it was like climbing toward the stars, into heaven. *You wanted us to find salvation and, in a way, I did.* I wasn't afraid anymore. I was tired and alive.

As I climbed that last step, a hollow sound escaped my lips. The trapdoor was open. The Grave yawned before me, seeming to grow larger and larger. I scanned the rows of empty stands.

"Father! I know you're out there!" My voice echoed, round and round in a circle. I climbed up onto the stage to see better. But I saw only the sky and the woods. The trees dug in their roots as if gathering their strength. Light-years away, a star winked.

The stage made me think, oddly, of my rehearsal that afternoon, and I recited the witches' lines loud and clear. " 'When shall we meet again? In thunder, lightning, or in rain? When the hurly-burly's done, when the battle's lost and won.' "

"Castley!" a voice called from the distance.

I trembled and turned to see Caspar racing up the steps. I raced down to him, because that was what the scene called for. I put my hands on either side of his face, pressing my thumbs into his soft, clean skin.

"You're here! I thought you were—"

"Where's Father?" he said.

I twisted my head toward the sky. "I don't know. He vanished."

"The police are here. They're calling Morty an ambulance."

Officer Dell Hardy appeared, marching sideways up the steps with his gun pointed down. "Where's the shooter?"

"Gone," I said.

"You kids go back to the parking lot. This is no place for children, you understand?"

Caspar lifted me down from the stage. We passed another officer on the steps. My feet crossed without my permission. The sudden calm purred like a buzz in my ears. My head felt light. *Look at all the pretty trees.* I took Caspar's hand. "How did you know we were here?"

"Momma. Momma told us," he said.

I caught myself on his chest. "She's alive?"

He looked away. "No. But I think she wanted . . ." He stopped and hummed to delay any tears. "She said she was sorry."

"No, she didn't."

"She should have."

We passed by a tree with a white star carved into the trunk. I pulled up short, wavered on my feet. Caspar held me tight. "What is it, Castella?"

"I never carved that." I lifted my finger, indicating the narrow star. "I'm sure of it. I would remember." I dove my finger into it, pressing the point so hard my finger pulsed.

"Someone else must've carved it," he said.

"But who? Who did it?"

He held me against him, so tight our hearts doubled. "Does it matter?"

"No." I sighed. "I guess it doesn't."

spring

We were on the roof again, helping clear Ms. Sturbridge's rain gutters. Ms. Sturbridge was making lemonade, even though it was barely spring and we were still in coats and jackets.

Mortimer was down below arguing with Uncle Michael about something he'd seen on TV. Hannan and Delvive were at church with Emily Higgins. Jerusalem was standing just below us with her easel, painting the house as we balanced on top of it.

If someone had told me six months ago that we would all be there together like that, I never would have believed it. I never could have seen it. But that's what life is like; it blinds you. It makes you think you'll never escape. But you will. You will if you keep fighting, even if sometimes you don't know what you're fighting for.

"The trees look so pretty, don't they?" Amity said, coming up behind me. "With all their new leaves?"

I shivered. I hadn't been thinking about the trees. I had been thinking about someone I knew who had disappeared. Disappeared, never to be found, dead or alive. I caught Caspar's eye and I knew he was thinking the same thing.

"Yes," I agreed. "They look pretty." I got back to work.

I used to think you were meant to learn something from everything, that life was one great big lesson, but I don't think that's true anymore.

I guard my mind and my heart, because you have to be careful what you learn; you have to be careful who you let in. Some people might look pretty or talk prettily, but it's the things they do that tell you if they're worthy of your time. It's the things they do that tell you if they deserve your faith.

acknowledgments

Lo + behold, god willing, you will get there to the other side of life and find happiness that every man craves, love, life + freedom.

—Alan Wass

I have to wonder what the point is in writing a thank-you to someone who will never read it, but wherever you are, in time or space or somewhere just outside it, this book wouldn't exist without you. I wouldn't exist without you, because I would be someone else, and thanks to you, I'm a better version of myself. You believed in me, you supported me, you inspired me, you drove me crazy, but most of all you loved me, all of me, for who I was and who I wanted to be, instead of what you wanted from me. This book, and everything I am, is for you, always.

Thank you to Hortensia Perez, who helped me send

my first book to a random Hollywood address we found online. I told you something would happen. Wish you were here to see it.

Thank you to my editor, Niamh Mulvey; my copy editor, Kate Hurley; my cover designer, Kate Gaughran; and the team at Quercus.

Thank you to my agents, Madeleine Milburn and Cara Simpson.

Thank you to my parents, Kit and Jim,

My siblings, Tim, Noah, Seth, Christina, Emma, Beverly, Colton, and Thomas,

My Brazier-in-laws, Carrie, Kiersten, Shayne, Josh, Brad, Nick, and Cassie,

My Brazier nephews and nieces, Elena, Lydia, Rocky, Boston, Jonah, Rachel, Abram, Nigel, Chase, Georgiana, Sienna, Charlie, Ezra, Eli, Peter, Henri Alan, and Grant,

And the Wass family, Chris, Angela, Mandy, Caroline, Alison, Vanessa, Fab, Josh, Lillie, Harry, and Leo,

For all their love and support.

A special thanks to EVERYONE I've connected with on Twitter. This book came together thanks to your support, advice, and critiques, sometimes in a DM, sometimes in a tweet. Thank you for teaching me that wherever I am, whatever I'm going through, there is always someone out there to talk to, to rant to, to share in this wonderful, torturous experience we call writing (and sometimes, by its lesser name, "life").

To the readers, I can't wait to hear from you. You're the reason I started writing to begin with (and the reason I wrote a shit-ton of fan fiction). All this publishing business is just a way to get this story to YOU.

I would also like to thank the future, for being just beyond our reach, and for tantalizing us with the possibilities of what we can one day be.

get to know eliza wass

What did you do before you became a writer?

I worked at Disneyland, then as a camp counsellor, as a children's tutor, a riding instructor, an actress, a waitress, bartender, bookseller, journalist, in real estate, in retail and accounting. I wanted to be a writer but I didn't have the confidence and I didn't understand the publishing industry.

My husband Alan Wass was very instrumental in my deciding to 'be a writer.' There was no disconnect for Alan between wanting to be a musician and actually being one; he just *was* a musician. I realized I needed to make writing my job before I had any of the perks like money or publication. Alan also believed in me, which is so, so important.

What do you think happens next for Castley and the other Cresswell siblings?
In my dream world I would write a sequel because, in my mind, the story is just beginning. What we are left with at the end of the novel is six children with no parents, an uncle they don't really know, and no settled personalities or solid trust between them. I think at least one would go back to living the way they were before, and that might give an insight into how their father ended up out in the woods in the first place.

I tried to give the story a sense of resolution, but of course these characters would continue to be affected by what happened to them for the rest of their lives, and I would like to see them triumph over that (in the only way people can – which is to say, never completely, but *mostly*).

What inspired you to write Castley's story?
There's this scene in the film *Walk the Line* where Johnny Cash is in the recording studio and the producer says something like 'if you could only sing one song that would

sum you up for the rest of your life, what would that song be?' So I was trying to write a book and I just thought, *What's the most important message I have to share with people*, and for me that was deciding to leave the religion I was raised in.

At that time, it was the most difficult thing I had ever done. So I took that situation and I amplified it to really bring across this message that you have to be true to yourself, even if no one is supporting you and maybe there isn't a 'happy ending' on the other side.

Are you working on anything new?
Yes. Somewhat eerily, the original story I pitched as part of my two-book deal was about a family struggling to deal with a death. Six months later my husband passed away which, needless to say, gave the story a much stronger resonance.

Hopefully this story pans out because I would like to be part of opening up a better dialogue about death. People are very hesitant to talk about death in society. There is this pervasive notion that it's 'depressing'—which, yes, it is, but it is also a lot of other things—and these attitudes only serve to further isolate those who are grieving. So I would very much like to open up a dialogue to better allow grieving people the chance to connect and find support.

I said above that in the past choosing my own religion was the most difficult thing I had ever done, but that has certainly changed now. I think death is one of the most intense subjects in the world; it's so powerful that people are actually afraid to talk about it. I would like to change that for the sake of the people who don't have a choice.

Tweet Eliza @Lovefaithmagic,
and look out for her next book,
coming Spring 2017